Hector MacLean

Ultonian Hero-Callads

Collected in the Highlands and Western Isles of Scotland...

Hector MacLean

Ultonian Hero-Callads
Collected in the Highlands and Western Isles of Scotland...

ISBN/EAN: 9783744728973

Printed in Europe, USA, Canada, Australia, Japan

Cover: Foto ©Andreas Hilbeck / pixelio.de

More available books at **www.hansebooks.com**

Ultonian Hero=Ballads

Collected in the Highlands and Western Isles of Scotland.

From the year 1516, and at successive periods till 1870.

Arranged; Corrected Metrically and Orthographically; and Translated into English

BY

HECTOR MACLEAN, M.A.I.

(Under the Auspices of the Islay Association.)

Glasgow:

ARCHIBALD SINCLAIR, Printer & Publisher,

10 Bothwell Street.

MDCCCXCII.

TO MY

ESTEEMED AND HONOURED FRIEND

John Crawfurd Graham, Esquire,

LAGAVULIN, ISLAY;

A GENTLEMAN CONNECTED WITH ISLAY

BY

BIRTH AND ANCESTRY;

A WARM FRIEND OF THE LATE

John F. Campbell, of Islay,

AND THE

TRUSTED PATRON OF ISLAYMEN EVERYWHERE:

THIS WORK IS DEDICATED

WITH THE AUTHOR'S PROFOUND RESPECTS.

PREFACE.

Professor Zimmer tells us that early Irish history
falls into three periods, the first reaching from pre-
historic times, to about the year 350, A.D., the second
to the end of the 7th century. No external activity on
the part of the Irish is recorded, during the first period;
the second, on the contrary, witnesses the harrying of
the coasts of Britain, the establishment of the kingdom
of Dalriada and the settlements in North and South
Wales; whilst the third period is filled by the wars of
the Northmen invaders. These historical periods are
reflected in the heroic sagas, the oldest of which are
concerned solely with intertribal conflicts, the heroes of
which do not leave Ireland, the topography of which is
coherent and accurate. The bulk of the sagas took
shape, however, in the second,—the Irish viking period
as it may be called. The heroes sally forth out of
Ireland, especially to the western seaboard of Scotland,
colonised as we know by the same Ulster tribes to whom

we owe the oldest heroic tales.   The third, or Norse period, has also left its mark on the sagas; allusion is made to Norway, Norse warriors appear as foes or allies of the Irish chieftains.   Nay more, a close examination of the sagas shows that they are in part corrupted by an admixture of elements derived from the Teutonic hero-tales.—*Archæological   Review,   Vol. ii. No. 2, p. 138.*

What relations Ireland had with foreign countries or how it was peopled we have nothing but fictitious and fabulous accounts.   Ethnological research has succeeded in ascertaining that the Iberian race constituted its population as well as that of Britain before the Celts arrived.

The inhabitants of Donegal county and Kerry, who are of smaller stature than the other Irish, and swarthy in complexion are considered to be descendants of those old Iberians; and for similar reasons, the southern Welsh.   The Spanish Basques from their stature and other physical characteristics are identified with them. The same race extended at one time from the north of Britain.   Another tall race fair or red-haired and white-skinned, extended from Africa, through Spain and France westwards to the British Isles. Professor Sayce speaks of this race in his book on the Hittites, pp. 15-17, "The Hittites and Amorites were therefore mingled together in the mountains of Palestine like the two races which ethnologists tells us, go to form the modern Kelt. But the Egyptian monuments teach us that they were of very different origin and character. The Hittites were a people with yellow skins and 'Mongoloid' features, whose receding foreheads, oblique eyes, and protruding upper jaws, are represented as faithfully on their own monuments as they are on those of Egypt, so that we cannot accuse the Egyptian artists of caricaturing their enemies. If the Egyptians have made the Hittites ugly, it was because they were so in reality. The Amorites, on the contrary, were a tall and handsome people. They are depicted with white skins blue eyes, and reddish hair, all the characteristics, in fact, of the white race. Mr. Petrie points out their resemblance to the Dardanians of Asia Minor, who form an intermediate link between the white-skinned tribes of the Greek seas and the fair complexioned Libyans of Northern Africa. The latter are still found in large numbers in the mountainous regions which stretch eastward from Morocco, and are usually known among the French under the name of Kabyles. The traveller who first meets with them in Algeria cannot fail to be struck by their likeness to a certain part of the population in the British Isles. Their clear-white freckled skins, their blue eyes, their golden-red hair and tall stature, remind us of the fair Kelts of an Irish village ; and when we find that their skulls, which are of the so-called dolichocephalic, or 'long-headed' type, are the same as the skulls discovered in the pre-historic cromlechs of the country they still inhabit, we may conclude that they represent the modern descendants of the white-skinned Libyans of the Egyptian monuments.

"In Palestine also we still come across representatives of a fair-complexioned blue-eyed race, in whom we may see the descendants of the ancient Amorites, just as we see in the Kabyles the descendants of the ancient Libyans. We know that the Amorite type continued to exist in Judah long after the Israelitish conquest of Canaan. The captives taken from the southern cities of Judah by Shishak in the time of Rehoboam, and depicted by him upon the walls of the great temple of Karnak, are people of Amorite origin. Their regular profile of sub-acquiline cast, as Mr. Tomkins describes it, their high cheek-bones and martial expression are the features of the Amorites, and not of the Jews.

" Tallness of stature has always been a distinguishing characteristic of the white race. Hence it was that the Anakim, the Amorite inhabitants of Hebron, seemed to the Hebrew spies to be as giants, while they themselves were but 'as grasshoppers' by the side of them (Numbers xiii. 33). After the Israelitish invasion remnants of the Anakim were left in Gaza and Gath and Ashkelon (Joshua xi. 22), and in the time of David Goliath of Gath and his gigantic family were objects of dread to their neighbours (2 Samuel xxi. 15·22).

"It is clear, then, that the Amorites of Canaan belonged to the same white race as the Libyans of Northern Africa, and like them preferred the mountains ·to the hot plains and valleys below. The Lybians themselves belonged to a race which can be traced through the peninsula of Spain and the western side of France into the British Isles. Now it is curious that wherever this particular branch of the white race has extended it has been accompanied by a particular form of cromlech, or sepulchral chamber built of large uncut stones. The stones are placed upright in the ground and covered over with other large slabs, the whole chamber being subsequently concealed under a tumulus of small stones or earth. Not unfrequently the entrance to the cromlech is approached by a sort of corridor. These cromlechs are found in Britain, in France, in Spain, in Northern Africa, and in Palestine, more especially on the eastern side of the Jordan, and the skulls that have been exhumed from them are the skulls of men of the dolichocephalic or long-headed type."

This race seems to be represented in early Irish romantic history by the Fomorians; for we find it mentioned that Partholon drove them out of Ireland. Madan Muinreamhar's four sons, Bog, Robhag, Ruibhne, and Rodan, were employed by Neimhidh to build a palace, and after having finished it he put them to death next morning. Rodan is both an Irish and a Scotch surname found in Galloway, *Gean* and *Geanann* were Fomorian chiefs who fell in battle with the sons of Neimhidh. Long thereafter *Gean* and *Geanann* were the names of two kings of the Firbolgs. Starn the son of Neimhidh fell by *Conoing* son of *Faobhar*, a Fomorian chief. *More* the son of *Deiliodh* was another chief among them. They latterly greatly oppressed the children of Neimhidh, and imposed heavy tributes on them. They had a female steward named *Liagh* who exacted the tribute. *Feathra* a king of the Fomorians was uncle to *Emer* the wife of Cuchullin. Balar of the blows, was also a king of the Fomorians and his wife *Cethlenn* was of the same race from whom Enniskilling *(Inis Chethlenn)* is named. *Kathleen* a modification of her name is a favourite Irish name. In Nott and Gliddon's "Types of Mankind" Mr. Gliddon compares the types of the Lybians and a kindred race that he saw on the monuments of Egypt with a type that abounds in the Highlands of Scotland. There is doubtless a type of tall, large bodied men found in the

Scottish Highlands, and in Ireland, not traceable to the Scandinavian or the Celt which would seem to have come from the South.

Professor Zimmer tells us that the second period of Irish history reaches from about the year 350, A.D. to the end of the 7th century; that the second period witnesses the harrying of the coasts of Britain, the establishment of the kingdom of Dalriada, and the settlements in North and South Wales.

When these Irish encountered the Romans first they were designated by the latter Scoti. How, therefore, did he Romans so name them? The Romans were generally desirous to know by what name any people they came in contact with called themselves, and as they more frequently made inquiry among the warriors of a tribe, so we generally find that the most of the names they gave to tribes both in Gaul and Britain, signify *warriors* in the various dialects of the different tribes In O'Davoren's Glossary, as published in Stokes' "Three Irish Glossaries," we find *Scath no Scoth = laoch*, *Scath* or *Scoth*, that is warrior. The *th* in *Scoth*, in the 4th century was probably a mute aspirate, and its plural was likely *Scothi* pronounced Scot-hi; so from this name the Romans would form Scoti, to suit their own tongue. The Irish at a later period, forgot and misunderstood the origin of the name Scoti, whence Scotia a name for Ireland, was formed.   The names Scuit (Scots), *Scot-bheulra*, (the Irish or Gaelic language,) were formed, and ultimately, the name Scotia was transferred to North Britain, because the Dalriadic colony in the Scottish Highlands, became the principal people there, and the Scottish colony in Galloway, and the neighbouring districts of Ayrshire, and Dumfriesshire, co-operated with the Dalriads of the North to form the modern Scottish nation.

The foremost among the oldest Irish manuscripts, are the two great vellums, the *Leabhar na h-Uidhre*, (L.U.) written down at the end of the 11th century, and Book of Leinster, (L.L.) written down in the middle of the 12th century.   All these MSS. are described in themselves as compilations from older MSS.   The second cycle of heroic tradition is found nearly entire in L.U. and L.L.   The annalistic work of Ireland can be traced back with certainty to the 11th century, gives, generally, both the pre-Christian and the Ultonian cycles as real history.   Tighernach the greatest of the early Irish annalists died in 1088, who alone raises doubts as to the nature of the record previous to the year 289 B.C.   The foundation of Emania by Cimbaoth is assigned by him to this year.   Modern scholars have followed him and have looked upon the earlier annals as fictitious.   The progress of the euhemerising process in the poems of Eochaid hua Flainn, who died in 984, and in those of Flainn Manistrech and Gilla Coemain, Irish translator of Nennius; the form- er died in 1056 and the latter in 1072, is to be observed. It attains its culmination in the *Leabhar Gabhala*, or book of Invasions, which is known to have been chiefly the work of Flainn Manistrech who was reputed in his day to be the most learned of native his- torical and antiquarian scholars. Chronology greatly took up his attention, and the complicated synchronism of the Irish annals, as regards the events of sacred and profane history, is to be traced to him more than to any other man. The non-historic character of these annals is sufficiently clear. It is different with the Ultonian cycle. The record is here so full, so marked with precision, and so detailed. It hangs together so coherent that at first considering it, it would seem im- possible to take it for anything else than what it assumes to be, an account of men and women that have really lived and of events that really happened. The acceptance of this part of the native annals by Tighernech, who gave proof of his independent and critical spirit by rejecting the earlier portion, has also spoken in its favour. At all events four of the scholars best qualified to give an opinion, Professors Windisch, Zimmer, Kuno Meyer, and Mr. Hennessy, have declared without hesitation in favour of the material correctness of these sagas. It is held by these learned and talented men that a real High-King of Ireland, *Connaire Mór,* a contemporary of Julius Cæsar, was slain by over-sea pirates as is related in the tale of Bruden da Derga ; that Conchobar did disposses his uncle Fergus of the chieftainship of Ulster, deceitfully killed the sons of *Uisnach,* and had to contend with the whole of Ireland in war, headed by Aillil and Medbh of Connaught who were aided by Fergus and other Ulster exiles. In this war Cuchullin took a conspicuous part, as is related in the tales of the Fate of the Sons of *Uisnach* and in the "*Táin bó Cuailgne,*" or the Raid for the Kine of Cooley ; and the numerous other tales respecting Cuchullin and his compeers which have been transmitted to us include a reflex of real fact. In reply to which it may be pointed out that Tighernach's testimony goes no further than that the euhemerising process was applied to the god-tales of the race at a much later date than to the hero-tales, a fact which could be paralleled with facility from other racial mythologies. The present annals proceed without interruption, so that it is not possible to lay the finger upon any set of events previous to the fourth century A.D. and assert " here fiction stops, here history commences." The partizans of the historic credibility of the Ultonian cycle look, as a rule, with a less favourable eye upon the Ossianic sagas. The greater portion of these are found in MSS. later by far than those in which the Ultonian cycle is obtained, and it is maintained that they are principally the product of late romantic fancy operating often upon themes and situations borrowed from the older heroic tales.

The large amount of Irish saga literature belonging to the Ultonian cycle dates, in its form, back to the tenth century, and there is MS. tradition of part of it extending back to the seventh century, different forms of the same saga can be discriminated as far back as there are means of research and these Sagas have undergone the same harmonising process but not the same euhemerising process as the earlier annals, the same medieval scholar was conspicuous in the one case as in the other. In writing the preceding part of this preface I have been guided by that able article by Mr. Alfred Nutt, "Celtic Myth and Saga." in No. 2 of the *Archæological Review.*

Some variants of the following ballads have been collected in the Highlands. Two of the variants here submitted are taken from Dean Macgregor of Lismore's Book; the Lay of the Heads and the Lay of Freich; the Lay of Conlach is taken partly

from the Dean's Book and partly from Gillies'
Collection of Gaelic Songs and Poems. The
transliteration of Dr. Mac Lauchlan is not accurately
executed as he has reduced the Gaelic to one dialect
of the language whereas the Gaelic of the Dean
consists of several subdialects belonging to various
districts of the Highlands, from natives of those districts.
There are also some expressions which Dr. Mac Lauchlan
did not know, translated erroneously, but it was a
difficult task to perform when he undertook it; even
the knowledge of the language has since immensely
extended, and great credit is unquestionably due to
him for what he did; which makes a very difficult book
easier for other students to throw light upon. From his
transcript I have transliterated and translated these
ballads. *An Garbh Mac Stairn* is a fusion of two
variants, the one in Mac Nicol's collection and the
other in Fletcher's collection, both collections in the
Advocates' Library, Edinburgh. We have both names
Garbh and *Starn* in early Irish history. Garbh the
son of Uthmhoir is mentioned at pp. 70 and 71 of
Joyce's Part I., Book I. of Keating's History of
Ireland, and *Starn* son of *Neimhidh* is mentioned at
pp. 88 and 89, *ibid.*

These ballads have been for many centuries sung and
rehearsed in the Highlands. There have been many

who could sing Fraoch till very lately in Islay. A few years ago Angus Mac Eachern often sang and rehearsed Conlach and many old Gaelic poems, but there are few left now in Islay who can sing old Gaelic ballads or rehearse old Gaelic poems. I give these ballads to the public with English translations expecting that in the rising young generation some will arise to do much better work than I have done, especially in the line of poetic translation.

HECTOR MACLEAN.

BALLYGRANT,
ISLAY, 1892.

AN CLAR-INNSIDH.

CONTENTS.

DUAIN ULTACH.

Duan a' Ghairbh Mhic Stairn.

DORSAIR.

1. "Eirich a Chú na Teamhra,—
Chi mi loingeas tha do-labhradh;—
Lom-lán, nan cuan clannach
Do loingeas mór nan allmharach!"

CONALL.

2. "Breugach thu dhorsair gu muadh:—
Breugach thu 'n diugh 's gach aon uair!
'S e th' ann loingeas mór nam magh,
'S e teachd chugainne g' ar cobhair."

B

DORSAIR.

3. "Tha aon laoch an dorus Teamhra,
   Am port an rígh gu ro-mheamnach ;
   Ag rádh gun gabhar leis gun ealla,
   'S gu gabh geall air fearaibh Eireann."

4. "Chuige mise," arsa Cu-riodh,
   Araon agus O' Conchair,
   Fear-dian taoibh ghil,
   'S Fraoch fial Mac Fiúghaidh,
   Aodh Mac Garadh a' ghlúin ghil,
   'S Caoilte ro-gheal Mac Rónain.

PORTER.

5. "Na tig air sin a Chu-riodh—
   Na cantair comhradh gun chlí ;
   Cha chomhraigear ris gun fhail
   Air ard rioghachd na h-Eireann.

6. "Chonnairc mise cóig catha deug
   Do dh' fhamhairibh as ni 'm breug ;
   Breth air a' Gharbh as Tír shoir,
   Am Maoigh Gallan nan comhrag."

7. 'N sin nar thubhairt Conall Cearnach,
   Sonn catha na Claoin Teamhrach ;

Cha teid mi fein ris a' m' ghuin,
'S cha mhó 's eólach mi mu chleasaibh."

8. An sin nar thuirt Maobh thall a staigh,
Inghean Ochaidh, flath na Féinne;
"Na leigibh oglach nan cath
Staigh do thaigh Teamhra nan righ-fhlath."

9. 'N sin nar thuirt Conall gu cóir,
Deagh mhac áluinn Eidirsgeoil;
"Cha bhi ri radh, a bhean,
Gun diúlt sinne ri aon fhear."

10. Leigeadh a staigh, an sin, am fear mór,
Gu prap, am fianuis an t-slóigh:
'S ionad tri cheud a staigh,
Chaidh a réiteachadh dha 's an tráth sin.

11. Thog Cuchulainn an sin a sgiath,
Air a mhaoidhlin bharra-liath;
Sheall Naois air a dha shleagh,
'S ghlac Conall a chlaidheamh.

12. Thug iad a staigh an sin dronnadh,—
Cheud do bhiadh agus do dhibh gun uirich,
G'a chaitheadh gus an fhear mhór,
A tháinig as an Esraidh.

13. Nuair bu sháthach am fear mór,
Agus a thug e treis air ól :
Thug e sealltainn air a null,
Air caogad mac righ mu thimchioll.

14. An sin nar thuirt Brichdean gu muadh—
Mac Mhic Cairbri fa 'n Chraoibh Ruaidh ;
Fearas 's faoilte dhuit gun fheall,
Am fianuis fearaibh Eireann !

CONALL.

15. "Macanachd Eireann uile dhuit 's an am-so,
A Bhrichdean Bharr-bhuidhe ;
Fad 's a bhios mise a' m' righ gu teann
Air ard rioghachd na h-Eireann."

BRICHDEAN.

16. "Bhrathainn-se dhuit na Braighdean,
Leis am faigheadh thu na táintean,
Bu leat Lugha Mac Cu-riodh
'S Fiabhaidh Mac Ghoraidh.

17. "Fear-dian taoibh ghil,
'S Fraoch fial Mac Fiúghaidh,
Aodh Mac Gharadh a' ghlúin ghil,
'S Caoilte ro-gheal Mac Rónan.

18. "Luagha, sgiath argumaid am blagh,
Deagh mhac Righ Laighean Lúbaidh,
Cormaig an luingis, gu muadh,
Mac Mhic Cairbri fa'n Chraoibh Ruaidh.

19. "Buinne borburra, nach borb a steach,
Buin leat, gu luath, o Fhearghuth."

20. Ghabhadh an sin na mic righ,
Ann an taigh Teamhra, gu fíor;
Agus chuireadh iad a muigh,
Do'n *Treun-fhear*—na fhianuis.

AN GARBH.

21. "Bheiream-sa briathar righ ann,
Fhearaibh áille na h-Eireann;
Nach téid mi fein ann am luing,
'S mi gun ghéill o Chuchulainn."

CUCHULAINN.

22. "Bheiream-sa briathar righ eile,
'S e labhair an t-ard chu armach;
Nach toir thu mo gheills' air muir,
'S mi féin ann a' m' bheatha.

23. "'S bodach thu bhidheann údlaidh,
'S olc thu fein, 's olc do mhuinntir,

'S ro-olc bean do thaighe ;
'S chan fheárr a' bean-mhuinntir ;
'S cha toir thu mo Ghéills' air sáil,
'S chan 'eil annad féin ach allbharach ! "

24. 'An sin, 'nuair dh 'éirich an da thriath,
     Le neart chlaidheamh agus sgiath ;
     Togadar an talamh táth,
     Le 'n troidhibh anns an uair sin.

25. B' iomadach buille fo bhile sgiath,
     'S fuaim clisniche ri cliar ;
     Fuaim lann aig gaoith nan gleann,
     Fo sgleó nan curaidh cho teann.

26. Seachd oidhchean agus seachd ló,
     Thug iad anns an iomad sgleó ;—
     An ceann an t-seachdamh ló
     Cha b' airde an Garbh air a' mhaoigh,
     Na Cuchulainn, a' ghaisge.

27. An ceann an t-seachdamh ló,
     Thug Cuchulainn beum dhó ;—
     'Sgoilt e, o bhruan gu bran,
     An sgiath eangach, órruidh.

GARBH.

28. " A Choinchulainn, aithnich triath ;—
Agamsa, cha mhair mo sgiath ;
Ach aon cheum teichidh, 'n oir na 'n iar,
Cha tug mi riamh 's mi 'm bheatha."

CUCHULAINN.

29. " Bheiream-sa briathar righ eile,
'Se labhair e—'n t-ard Chu iorghuil ;—
" 'N t-aon cheum teichidh, siar na soir,
Chan 'eil fuidh d' roghainn a dhéanadh."

30. Thilg Cuchulainn uaidh a sgiath,
Air an fhaiche, oir as iar ;—
Ga b' eineach siod, b' olc an fhaoil,
Le maithibh uaisle na h-Eireann.

31. Ach thug Cuchulainn beum eile,
Le móid a mheamnaidh 's a sgeinidh ;
Togadar an lámh leis an lainn,
'S sgarar ceann o 'n cholainn.

CONALL.

32. " Macanachd Eireann uile
Dhuitse uamsa," arsa Conall ;
" 'S a' cheud chorn gun fheall
Ann am fianuis fearaibh Eireann."

CUCHULAINN.

33   "Rinn mise gníomh air Giolla nan Cuan,—
Creideadh an righ mar is dual ;—
Tha leaba aon laoich 'n so, a bh' air Cuan,
Tha 'n diugh gun aiseag le iomairt sluaigh,
A thriall gu taigh Teamhra nan righ-fhlath
Ghabhail géill air fearaibh Eireann."

Na Cinn.

Ughdar so CONALL CEARNACH *Mac Eddirschol.*

EIMHIR.

1. " A Chonaill, cha sealbh na cinn—
   Deimhin leam gu r' dheargas t' airm ;—
   Na cinn do chitheam air a' ghad,
   Sloinntear leat na fir fo 'm faoibh."

CONALL.

2. " A nighean Fhorgaill nan each—
   A Eimhir óig nam brigh binn ;
   'S ann an éirig chon nan cleas,
   Thugas leom a níos na cinn."

EIMHIR.

3. " Co an ceann mollach, dubh, mór—
   Deirge na 'n rós a ghruaidh ghlan ;
   Is e is goire do 'n leth chlí—
   An ceann diubh nach d' atharraich dath."

CONALL.

4. " Ceann righ Midhe nan each luath,"
   Arsa Mac Cairbre nan goith cam ;
   " An éirig mo dhaltain féin,
   Thugas leam an céin a cheann."

5. " Co 'n ceann ud air m' aghaidh thall,
    Go folt fann gu mall, sliom ;
    Rosg mar éire, deud mar bhláth ;
    Ailde no gach cruth a cheann."

6. " Manadh, b' e fear nan each,—
    Macamh Aoife do chreachadh gach cuan ;
    D' fhágas a cholann gun cheann,
    Is do thuit uile leam a shluagh."

7. "Co an ceann so ghabhas tu a' d' laimh,
    A Chonaill mhóir na báigh linn;
    O nach maireann Cu nan cleas,
    Ciod bheireadh thu air leas a chinn?"

8. "Ceann Mhic Fhearghuis nan each,—
    Bheireadh e cíth gach gurt;
    Mac mo pheathar an túir sheang,
    Do sgaras a cheann r' a chorp."

9. "Co an ceann ud shear, an fhuilt fhinn,
    Da ghreadadh na cinn go laimh ;

Fhuaireas aithne air a ghuth,—
Gun robhadar seal d' a réir."

CONALL.

10. "Síos an sud do thuit an cú—
Do rad a chorp fa chruth deas ;—
Cú Mac Coin, righ nan rann,
Thugas leam a cheann tar éis."

EIMHIR.

11. "Co an da cheann so is faide mach.
A Chonaill mhóir a bhráth bu bhinn ;
Air ghráidh t' aithne na ceil oirnn,
Ainm nam fear a ghuin na h-airm ?"

CONALL.

12. "Ceann Laoghaire is clar Chuilt,
An da cheann do thuit le m' ghuin ;
Do ghuin sud Cuchulainn chearn,—
Suinn dheargas m' airm 'n am fuil."

EIMHIR.

13. "Co an da cheann so is faide soir,
A Chonaill mhóir gach geal gníomh ?
Ionnan dath air folt nam fear,—
Deirge an gruaidh na fuil laoigh."

CONALL.

14. "Cullain bréagh is Cunnlaid cruaidh—
Dithis do bheireadh buaidh le feirg ;—

A Eimhir : siod soir an cinn—
D' fhágas an cuirp fa linne dheirg."

EIMHIR.

15.   " Co na sé cinn so is olc méin,
Do chitheam féin air m' aghaidh thuath ;
Gorm an aghaidh, dubh am folt,
O thilleadh rosg Chonaill chruaidh ?"

CONALL.

16.   " Seisear eascairdean a chú,—
Clann Chatleidin nam buadh gnáth ;—
Is iad sud an seisear laoch
A thuit leam, 's an airm a' m' laimh."

EIMHIR.

17.   " A Chonaill mhóir, athair rígh,
Co 'n ceann ud do 'n géilleadh cath ?
Gur órbhuidhe trillis o cheann—
Con comhdach sliom dh' airde bheart."

CONALL.

18.   " Ceann Mhic Finn, Mhic Rois ruaidh,
Mhic Nic Cní, fhuair bás le m' neart ;
A Eimhir ! is e so a cheud—
Ard righ Laighean nan lann breac ! "

EIMHIR.

19. "A Chonaill mhóir, mugh an sgeul,—
Creud a thuit, le d' laimh, gun lochd,
Do'n t-sluagh eagnuidhthe a bheil 'n sin,
An dioghaltas cinn a' chon?"

CONALL.

20. " Deichnear is seachd fichead ceud—
Deiream péin is áireamh slóigh—
Do thuit leamsa druim air dhruim,
Do nimh mo chuilg cunnla, rag."

EIMHIR.

21. "A Chonaill, cionnas ta iad—
Mnai Inse-fáil déisne a' choin ;
Cumha a mhic shamhailt tha,
Na bheil aca féin, air 'foir?"

CONALL.

22. "A Eimhir, ciod a dheanadh mi,
Gun mo chú am' réir 'san socht,
Gun mo dhaltan fa mhaith cruth,
A' dol bhuam am mugha an nochd."

EIMHIR.

23. "A Chonaill, tog mi 'san fheart,—
Tog mo leachd os leachd a' chon,

Os d' a chumhadh rachaim eug,—
Cuir mo bheul ri beul a' chon."

24.   " Is mi Eimhir a 's caoine dealbh—
Ni faighinn searbh dhioltadh dhomh
Do dheur nochan 'eil mo spéis,—
Truagh m' fhuireach air éis a Chon."

Cucbulainn 'n a Charbad.

" Cia fath do thurais, no do sgeul ? "
" Fath mo thurais is mo sgeul,
'Feara 'Eireann sud mar chímear,
Air teachd chugaibh air a' mhagh,
   An carbad air am bheil an dual fioghiordha fionda,
Air a dheanadh gu lùthmhor, lámhach, taiceil,
Far am bu lùghmhor, 's far am bu láidir,
'S far am bu lán-ghlic am pobull úr,
'S a' chathair fhrasanta randa :—
Caol, cruaidh, clocharra, colbhuidh ;—
Ceithir eich chliabh-mhor 's a' chaomh charbad sin.
   Ciod a chímear 's a' charbad sin ?
Na h-eich bhailg-fhionn, chailg-fhionn chluas-bheag,
Slios-tana, bas-tana, eachmhor, steudmhor,
Le sreunaibh chaol, lainnire, líomharra,
Mar léig, no mar chaoir-theine dheirg ;
Mar ghluasad laoigh chreuchta maoislich ;
Mar fharum ghaoithe, chruaidhe, gheamhraidh,
Teachd chugaibh anns a' charbad sin :
   Ciod a chímear 's a' charbad sin ?
   Chímear 's a' charbad sin,
Na h-eich liatha, lughmhor, stuadhmhor, láidir,
Threismhor, stuadhmhor, luathmhor, taghmhor

A bheireadh sparradh sgeiribh na fairge as an
    carraigibh—
Na h-eich mhearganta, thargaideach, threiseadach ;
Gu struthmhor, lughmhor, dearsa fhionn ;
Mar spuir iolaire ri gnúis ana-bheathaich ;
D'an goirear an Liathmhor mhaiseach,
Mheachtroigh mhór mhuirneach.
    Ciod a chímear 's a' charbad sin ?
    Chímear 's a' charbad sin
Na h-eich chinn-fhionn, chroidh-fhionn, chaolchasach,
Ghrinn-ghruagach, stobhradach, cheannardach,
Shról-bhreideach, chliabh-fharsuinn ;
Bheag-aosda, bheag-ghaoisdneach, bheag-chluasach,
Mhór-chridheach mhór-chruthach, mhór-
    chuinneanach,
Seanga, seudaidh, is iad searrachail ;
Bréagha, beadarra, boilsgeanta, baoth-leumnach,
D'an goireadh iad an Dubh-seimhlinn.
    Ciod a bhiodh 'na shuidhe 's a' charbad sin ?
    Bhiodh 'na shuidhe 's a' charbad sin,
An laoch cumaiseach, cumhachdach, deagh-fhoclach,
Líobharra, loinnearra, deagh-mhaiseach,
Tha seachd scallaidh air a rosg ;
'S air leinn gur maith am fradharc dha ;
Tha sé meoir chnámhach, reamhar
Air gach laimh tha teachd o ghualainn ;

Tha seachd fuilteana fionn air a cheann ;
Folt donn ri tointe a chinn,
'S folt sleamhuinn, dearg, air uachdar,—
'S folt fionn-bhuidhe air dhath an óir,
'S na faireill air a bhárr 'ga chumail ;
D'an ainm, Cuchulainn mac Seimh-suailti,
Mhic Aoidh, mhic Aigh, mhic Aoidh eile.
Tha eudann mar dhrithleana dearga :—
Lughmhor air leirg, mar luath-cheathach sléibhe,
No mar luathas éilde faonaich,—
No mar mhaigheach air machair-máil,
Gum bu cheum tric—ceum luath—ceum múirneach,—
Na h-eacha a teachd chugainn,—
Mar shneachd ri snoigheadh, nan sliosaibh ;—
Ospartaich agus unaghartaich
Nan eachaibh gu t' ionnsuidh.

C

Deirdri.

Fletcher's variant from his Collection in the Advocates' Library. This poem was taken down in 1750 from the dictation of a man who could neither read nor write.

Air bhith do rígh Eireann, Conchar, a' dol a phósadh ban-righ d' am b' ainm Deirdri, agus ag ullachadh air son na bainnse, mharbh iad laogh óg. Bha sneachd air úr-chur 'na luidhe air a ghrunnd 'san am. Dhóirt iad fuil an laoigh a muigh air an t-sneachda agus luidh fitheach air an fhuil. Bha Deirdri a' sealltuinn a mach air uinneig aig an am. Chunnairc i 'm fitheach ag ol na fola, agus thuirt i ris an righ ;— "Nach bu mhaiseach an duine aig am bitheadh a chneas cho geal ris an t-sneachda, a ghruaidh co dearg ris an fnuil, agus (holt co dubh ris an fhitheach." Fhreag-air an righ, ag radh gun robh clann peathar aige-san, agus gun robh h-aon diubh air an robh gach buaidh a dh 'ainmich i. Thubhairt Deirdri ris an righ a ríst nach cuireadh i cos 'na leabaidh gus am faiceadh i an duine sin. Air an aobhar sin chuir an righ fios air. Tháinig e féin agus a dha bhráthair. Agus do b'e an ainmeannan Naois, Aille, agus Ardan.

Air do Dheirdri Naois fhaicinn líonadh i le gaol dha, ionnas gun d' fhalbh i leis, agus dh' fhág i an righ. Dh' fhalbh Naois agus a dha bhráthair air long, agus sheol iad gus an deachaidh iad air tír aig Beinn Aird Agus bha giolla beag 'nan cuideachd d' am b 'ainm an Gille Dubh, a bha na chomhdhalta dhaibh, agus a' feith-eamh orra.

Duan Dheirdri.

1. Tur gun deachaidh iad air tuinn,
   Clann Uisneachan, a Dubh-Lochlann;
   Dh' fhág iad Déirdri 'san Gille Dubh
   Am Beinn Aird 'nan aonarain.

2. C' áite an cualas dán b'u duileadh,
   Na 'n Giolla Dubh ri dúr shuiridh,
   Air Déirdri Chruinneagach gheal.

AN GIOLLA DUBH.

"Bu chuibhte orm as ort bhith cuideachd."

DEIRDRI.

3. "Cha bu chuibhte mi us tu,
   Ghiollan Duibh nam miorún;
   Ach gus an tig' dhachaidh slán,—
   Clann Uisneachan a Dubh-Lochlann."

AN GIOLLA DUBH.

4. " Ge b'eug a rachadh tu dheth,
   'S ge d' fhaigheadh thu bás gun chumhadh ;
   Bithidh tu as Iain dubh an aon leabaidh,
   Gus an téid úir air do leachdainn.

5. " Gheibheadh thusa, Dheirdri ghuanach,
   Bhuamsa air mhadainn a máireach ;—
   Gheibheadh tu bainne 'chruidh chraobhaich
   Agus maorach a Inis-aonaich.

6. "Gheibheadh tu muinealan mhuc,
   Mar sin, agus sruthaga sheann-tuirc ;
   Gheibheadh tu braoideach as bó,—
   'S a laoigh mhín na fuilinn an so."

DEIRDRI.

7. "Ged gheibhinn uait caolaich fhiadha,
   Agus bradain bhroinne gheala ;
   B' annsa leam bior-chul-chas
   A laimh Naois Mhic Uisneachan.

8. " B 'e Naois a phógadh mo bheul,—
   Mo cheud fhear 's mo cheud leannan ;
   B' e Aille leigeadh mo dheoch,
   'S b' e Ardan a cháireadh m' adhart."

9. Ach súil gun tug Déirdri ghuanach,
   Mach air barr a' bhaile bhraonaich ;—

DEIRDRI.

" 'S áluinn an triuir bhráithre chi mi,—
'Snámhaidh iad na cuantan thairis.

10. " Tha Ard as Aille air an stiúir
    A' seóladh gu h-ard-rámhach, ciúin ;
    Mo ghrádh an geal-lámhach, geal !
    Tha m' fhear féin 'ga stiúradh siod.

11. " Ach smid na tigeadh air do bheul,
    Ghiollain Duibh nam braon sgeul ;
    Mu marbhar thu gun chionta dheth,
    As nior mó a chreidear mise.

12. " O ! Chlainn Uisneachan nan each,
    A tháinig a tír nam fear fuileach ;
    An d' fhuiling sibh táir bho neach ? .
    No ciod e so bha 'gur cumail ? "

CLANN UISNEACHAN.

13. " Bha 'gar cumailne mach uaitse ;—
    'S ann duinne gum b' fhuileach an ruaig—
    Righ Mac Rosnaich, ceann fear Fáil,
    Air ar glacadh 's air ar diongmhail."

14.   " C' áite an robh ur n-airm ghaisge,
      'S 'ur lámhan tapaidh fuileach ;
      Nuair a dh' fhuiling sibh—sibh féin s'án—
      Do Mhac Rosaich bhith 'gur diongmhail ?"

CLANN UISNEACHAN.

15.   " Cadal gun d' rinn sinn 'nar luing,—
      An triuir bhráithre druim ri druim ;
      M' an d' fhairich sinn beud na feall,
      Dh' iath na sé-longa-deug umainn."

DEIRDRI.

16.   " Cha bu mhise nach d' innis dhuibhse,
      A Chloinn Uisneachan bho b' ionmhuinn ;
      Nach bu lámh air bhlonaga ban,—
      'S nach bu shurd air cogadh, cadal."

CLANN UISNEACHAN.

17.   " 'S ged nach biodh cogadh fo 'n ghréin,
      Ach duine fada a thír féin ;
      Cadal fada 's beag a thlachd
      Do dhuine, is e air deórachd.

18.   " Deórachd, 's mairg d' am biodh an dán,—
      Gur gnáthach leatha cuid sheachrain ;—
      'S beag a h-urram, is mór a smachd,—
      Is mairg duine d' an dán deórachd.

19. " Ach chuir iadsan ann sin sinn,
An uamha shalaich fui thalmhainn ;
Far an tigeadh fódhainn an sáile,
Tri naoi uairean gach aon lá.

20. " Ach aon inghean mhaith bh' aig an rígh,—
Ghabh i dhinne móran truaghais ;
Seicheachan a h-athar gu léir—
Bu lionmhor ann bian éilde is aidhe—
Chuir i eadar sinn 's am fuar uisg' ;—
An righinn úr, o 's i b' fhearr tuigse ;
Ach do bhiodh a h-athair 's a' Chraoibh Ruaidh,
'Sa chairdean gu léir mu thimchioll."

AN RIGH.

21. " Teachd mo chagair a Thiormhail,
Chan 'eil rúine nam ban maith—
Innsidh 's a' chúil na chluinn iad."

TIORMHAIL.

22. " Ciod an rúine a bhiodh ann
Nach innseadh tu do t' aon inghin ?
'S an rúine a gheibhinnse uait,
Gun gleidhinn bliadhna, gu dil,
Fui bhile mo chíche deise ;
'S an rúine gheibhinn bho chách,
Athair ghráidh ! gun innsinn duitse.'

AN RIGH.

23. " Chuir rígh Eireann fios, air sáil,
Dh' ionnsuidh uaislean Bharr-Fáil,
Gum faiginn-sa lán mo luinge
Do dh' ór 's do dh' innsridh, 's do dh' ionmhas,
Chionn na ciomaich chur, gun fheall,
Air chuan na h-Eireann am máireach."

24. Ach leig an inghean osna throm
As a cridhe gu ro mhór;
Fhreagair aisnichean an taighe
Leis an osann leig an inghean.

AN RIGH.

25. " Co so leig an osann throm ?—
Gur duilich leo na ciomaich."

TIORMHAIL.

" 'S mise leig an osann throm—
Do chiomaich gur coma leam.

26. "Tha earrann mhór ann a' m' thaobh clí
'S gum marbhadh i caogad rígh;
'S tha luain mhór air mo chridhe,
'S an taobh eile, ma choinneamh na h-earrainn."

27. Ach tháiniʒ i chugainn d' ar fios,
An Tiormhail bu ghile cneas.

CLANN UISNEACHAN.

" An robh thu anns an dún ud thall?
No ciod an aithris a th' ann oirnne ? "

TIORMHAIL.

28. " Bha mise anns an dún ud thall,
'S is truagh an aithris a th' ann oirbhse ;—
Gum faigh m' athair lán a luinge
. Do dh' ór, do dh' innsridh, 's do dh' ionmhas;
Chionn na ciomaich chur, gun fheall,
Air chuan na h-Eireann am máireach."

29. " Ach sínibh chugamsa bhur casan,
As gun tomhais mi na glasan ;
Nach fhág mi bonn diubh air dearmad
Air fad, air leud, na air doimhnead."

30. Ráinig ise an ceard Cluanach,—
Fhuaras órd gobha 'na laimh,
As e 'ga shíor bhualadh air innein.

AN CEARD CLUANACH.

31. " Is neónach leam thu nighean rígh,
Bhith falbh oidhche 'n am chadail."

TIORMHAIL.

"'S e bheireadh dhomhsa bhith falbh oidhche,
Cóir m' fhoighneachd a bhith agad."

AN CEARD CLUANACH.

32. "'S néarachd mise bhith beó,
'S coir a fhoighneachd a bhith agam :—
'S an ceann dubh so th' air mo bhrághad,
Gur tu rinn dhomhsa ghleidheadh.

33. "Bha mi lá a' pronnadh óir,
An ceardach t' athar an Cluanaidh ;
Choinnicheadh ormsa 'n t-ór a ghoideadh,
'S gum bu sgeul siod air námhaid."

TIORMHAIL.

34. "'S i 'n fhail óir, thug mise dhuit,
Chum an ceann air do bhráighe.

35. "Mire gun d' rinneas a' m' luing,
Air onfhadh na mara thruim ;
Thuit iuchraichean m' athar thar bórd,—
'S truagh gun mise 'nan sruth-lorg ! "

36. Ach dh' éirich e suas, an ceard Cluaineach,·—
Mac an t-saoir as a' Chraoibh Ruaidh ;

Is rinn e na tri iuchraiche buadhach,
Ri aiteal na h-aon leth-uaire.

AN CEARD CLUANACH.

37. " Na tigeadh smid as do bheul—
Moch, no anmoch, no ma fheasgar ;
Nach gun labhair an teintein dubh sin,
Na 'n t-innein air an deach an déanamh."

38. Ach thainig i rís d' ar fios—
An Tiormhail nan ciabha cleachdach.

TIORMHAIL.

39. " Sínibh chugamsa bhur casan,
As gum fuasgail mi na glasan ;
Mur dh' fhág mi bonn diubh air dearmad,
Air fad, air leud, no air doimhnead."

40. Ach thog Naois a chos ri eallachain,
Ard is Ailie co-fhearr-luath.

TIORMHAIL.

41. "An triuir bhráithrean bu mhaith diongmhail ;—
Bheil sibh nise air 'ur cois ?
No bheil a bhos na ni 'ur diongmhail ? "

CLANN UISNEACHAN.

42. " No 'm bitheadh againn ar trí chlaidhmhean,
     Agus lón chúig oidhchean ;
     Solus céire leth mar leth,
     'S gum bu léir dhuinn aghaidh a chéile."

43. Chaidh i dh' iarraidh nan trí chlaidhmhean ;—
     Cha b' e faoidh a b' fhusa dheanamh;
     Ráinig i Gille an t-seómair—
     An ríghinn úr m' an iadh an t-ómar.

AN GILLE SEOMAIR.

44. " S neónach leam, a nighean rígh,—
     Bhith falbh oidhche 'n am chadail ; "—

TIORMHAIL.

     " 'S e bheireadh dhomh bhith falbh oidhche,
     Cóir m' fhoighneachd a bhith agad."

45. " Na déanamsa ceartas díonaidh—
     Nighean an righ o Dhun Meara ;
     Tha mi 'g iarraidh nan tri claidhmhean,
     Agus lón chúig oidhchean ;
     Solus céire leth mar leth,
     'S gum bu léir dhuinn aghaidh a chéile."

AN GILLE SEOMAIR.

46. " Ciod a dheanadh tu do chlaidheamh,
     A nighean rígh ard-fhlathail ;

'S nach b' urrainn thu chur leis catha,
No thoirt leis latha seirbhis ? "

TIORMHAIL.

47. " Bheirinn claidheamh dhiubh mar *ghit*,
Do mhac a fhuair rígh ri ríghinn;—
Bheirinn claidheamh eile dhiubh
Do cheud marcach nan each ciuin.

48. " Bheirinn claidheamh eile dhiubh,
Do ard mharascail mo luinge."
Leag i na naoi *piosan* óir
Air a' bhord air son nan tri claidhmhean.

CLANN UISNEACHAN.

49. " Thug i chugainn ar tri chlaidhmhean,
Agus lón chúig oidhchean,
Seorsa céire leth mar leth,
'S gum bu léir dhuinn aghaidh a chéile."

50. Sin gur thainig g' ar fios—
An Tiormhail bu gile cneas ;—

TIORMHAIL.

" Tha long aig m' athair-se air sál,
Roimhe thall air Chluan Ciaran.

51. " Cúigear a' gleidheadh na luinge,—

Aon fhear mór os gach duine,
'S gun diongadh e ceud an comhrag.

52. " Ach ma theid sibhse 'na dháil,
Gun eagal na gun fheall-sgáth ;
Buailibh gu cothromach, ceart,
Bhur tri chlaidhmhean 'na aon alt."

CLANN UISNEACHAN.

53. " Ge bu dorcha dubh an oidhche,
Bu neo-bhorb a rinn sinn iomramh ;
Bhuail sinn gu cothromach, ceart,
Ar tri chlaidhmhean 'na aon alt.

54. " Thig thusa steach a' d' luing,
A Thiormhail, a' s ionmhuinne leinne ;
As aon bhean cha teid os do cheann,
Ach aon bhean 's an tír a'n téid thu."

TIORMHAIL.

55. " Ciod an aon bhean a bhiodh ann,
'S gur mi choisiun dhuibh na h-anamzim ?
B'uaibhreach dhomhsa sin a dheanamh,—
'S a liuthad mac righ tha 'ga m' iarraidh ;—
Na 'n triallainn air cheumannan cas,
Air sgáth buidhne coimhiche."

CLANN UISNEACHAN.

56. " Leubhaidh iad ort, A Gheal Shoilleir,—
Mu as fíor gu bheil thu torrach ;—
Ma 's mac na inghean a bhios ann,
Luaidhear air fearaibh na h-Eireann e."

TIORMHAIL.

57. " 'S aon nighean mi do 'n righ,—
'S mothaid dheth sud mo phrís ;—
Ach 's olc an saothraiche, re seal,
Nach tugadh aon eun an caladh.

58. " Ach fanaidh mi bliadhna air do ghaol,
Agus bliadhna eile chion t' iomraidh ;—
'N ceann na cuigeamh na seathamh bliadhna,
Thig 'ga m' iarraidh 'n sin air m' athair,
'S gleidhidh mise do shíth dhuit
Bho rígh an domhain 's bho Chonchobhair."

PAIRT II.

Caoidb Dheirdri.*

Agus air innseadh na nitheadh dhoibh, bha Déirdri ro-
dhiomach dhiubh, chionn gun d' fhág iad Tiormhail
'n an déigh, agus air son a feabhas dhoibhsan nach
iarradh ise os a cionn gu bráth.   An sin ghabh
Déirdri agus iadsan an turas a rís g' a iarraidh, agus
chunnairc ise aisling.

DEIRDRI.

1.   " Aisling a chunnaic mi 'n raoir,
       Air triuir mhac rígh Barrachaoil ;
       Bhith 'g an cuibhreachadh 's 'gan cuir 's an uaigh;
       Le Conchobhar as a' Chraoibh Ruaidh."

CLANN UISNEACHAN.

2.   " Ach leag thusa t' aisling, a Dhéirdri,
       Air aonach nam bruthaichean arda,
       Air maraichean na fairge muigh,
       'S air na clochaibh garbha, glasa ;—
       'S gum faigh sinne síth, 's gun tabhair,
       Bho rígh an Domhain 's bho Chonchobhair."

*Caoidh Dhéirdri here is from Stewart's Collection of Gaelic
Songs and Poems, being a part of *Aoidheadh Chlainn
Uisnich* in that work.

3. " Ach co moch 's a tháin' an ló,
'S a sgaoileadh bho 'r cúl an ceó ;
C' áite an do ghabh ar loingeas tír,
Ach fui dhorus an ard-rígh."

4. Tháinig Conchar féin a mach,
'S naoi ceud deug sluaigh leis ;
'S dh' fheóraich e gu breagha, bras,
Co iad na slóigh so th' air an loingeas ?

CLANN UISNEACHAN.

5. " S iad clann do pheathar féin a t' ann,
Is iad 'nan suidhe 'n cathair aingis."

CONCHAR.

6. " Cha chlann peathar dhomhsa sibh,
'S chan e gníomh a rinn sibh orm ;
Ach mo nárachadh le feall,
Ann am fiadhnais fir na h-Eireann."

CLANN UISNEACHAN.

7. " Ciod ged thug sinn uait do bhean—
Deirdri chruinneagach, ch*ruinn-lamh, gheal ;
Rinn sinn riut báigh bheag eile,
'S b' e 'n tráths' am a cuimhneachaidh.

8. " 'N latha sgáin do long air sáile,
'S i lán do dh' ór is do dh' airgiod ;

D

Thug sinne dhuits' ar long fhéin,
'S shnámh sinn *fhéin* cuan mu d' thimchioll."

CONCHAR.

9. " Ge d' dheanadh sibh rium caogad báigh,
Air mo bhuidheachas gu fíor ;
Bhur síth, chan fhaigheadh sibh an teinn,
Ach gach aon díth bu mhó gum faodainn."

CLANN   UISNEACHAN.

10. " Rinn sinn báigh bheag cile riut,
'S b' e 'n tràths' am a cuimhneachaidh ;
'N latha mheath an t-each breac ort,
Air faiche Dhun-Dealgain ;
Nois, thug sinne dhuit an t-each glas,
Bheireadh gu bras thu 'n t-slighe."

CONCHAR.

11. " Ge d' dhéanadh sibh rium caogad báigh,
Air mo bhuidheachas gu fíor ;
Bhur síth chan fhaigheadh sibh an teinn,
Ach gach aon díth bu mhó gum faodainn."

CLANN   UISNEACHAN.

12. " Do rinneamar dhuit báigh bheag eile,
O 's e nis an t' am d' a cuimhneachaidh ;—

Chuir sinn thu 'n comainean líonmhor,—
'S díleas ar cóir air do chomraich !

13. " An t' am do chuir Murchadh Mac Brian,
Na seachd cathaibh am Binn Eadair,
Thug sinn chugad, gun easbhuidh,
Cinn mhac righ na h-Earradheise."

CONCHAR.

14. " Ge d' dhéanadh sibh rium caogad báigh,
Air mo bhuidheachas gu fíor ;
Bhur síth chan fhaigheadh sibh an teinn,
Ach gach aon dìth bu mhó gum faodainn."

DEIRDRI.

15. " Eirich a Naois is glac do chlaidheamh,
A dheagh mhic an rìgh a' s glan coimhead ;
Creud fa 'm faigheadh an cholann shuairc,
Ach a mháin aon chuairt do 'n anam."

16. Chuir Naois a shálta ri clár,
Is ghlac e chlaidheamh 'na dhorn ;
'S bu gharg deannal nan laoch
'Tuiteam air gach taobh do bhord.

17. Thorchair mic Uisnich 's a' ghreis,
Mar thri gallain a' fás co dheas,

Air an sgrios le doinionn éitidh—
Ni 'n d' fhág meangan, meur, na geug dhiubh.

18. " Cha bhás leam a nis 'ur bás,
     A Chloinn Uisneachan gun aois ;
     O na thuit e leibh, gun fheall,
     Treas marcaich uasal na h-Eireann."

CONCHAR.

19. "Gluais a Dhearduil as do luing,—
     A Gheug úr an abhra dhuinn ;
     As chan eagal do d' ghnuis ghlain,
     Fuath, na eud, na achasan."

DEIRDRI.

20. " Cha téid mise mach as mo luing,
     Gus am faigh mi mo rogha athchuinge ;
     Cha tír, cha talamh, as cha tuar,
     Cha triuir bhráithre bu ghloine snuadh ;
     Chan ór, 's chan airgiod, 's chan eich—
     Ni mó as bean uaibhreach mise—
     Ach mo chead a dhol do 'n tráigh,
     Far am bheil Clann Uisnich 'nan támh`
     As gun tugainn na tri póga meala,
     Do 'n tri chorpaibh caomha, geala."

21. Dh' fhuasgail iad a folt donna-bhuidhe tláth
    M' an cuairt do 'n righinn coimh-réidh,—
    A h-eudach gu barraibh a cos,
    M' an tugadh i leatha 'm braid,
    Cothrom cró na snáthaide ;—
    Ach aon fhail óir a 'bha mu 'meur—
    'S ann a chuir i sud 'na beul,—
    As dh' imich i leis do 'n tráigh,
    Far an robh Clann Uisneachan,—
    As fhuair saor a' snoigheadh rámh—
    A sgian aige 'na leath laimh,
    'S a thuadh aige 's an laimh eile.

DEIRDRI.

22. "A shaoir a's fearr d' am facas riamh,
    Creud air an tiubhradh tu an sgian ?
    Is e a bheirear dhuit, d' a ceann,
    Aon fháine buadhach, na h-Eireann,"

23. Shanntaich an saor am fáine,—
    Air a dheisead as air 'áillead ;—
    Thiubhradh do Dhearduil an sgian,
    Agus ráinig i ionad a miann.

24. Dh' imich i an sin do 'n tráigh ;
    Far an robh Clann Uisneachan ;

'S fhuair i 'n sin gun agadh.
An tri chuirp sínte síos co fada.

DEIRDRI.

25.   " Cha gháirdeachas gun Chlann Uisnich
O ! is túrsach gun bhith 'n 'ur cuallach ;—
Tri mic rígh le 'n dioltadh deóraich,
Tha gun chomhradh re h-uchd uaighe.

26.   " Tri mathghamhna Inse Breatain,—
Triuir sheabhac o Shliabh a' Chuilinn ;
An triuir dh' an géilleadh na gaisgich,
As dh' an tiúbhradh na h-amhais urram.

27.   " Na tri eoin a b' áillidh snuadh,
A tháinig thar chuan nam bárc ;
Triuir mhac Uisnich o 'n Charra chruinn,—
Tri lachaibh air tuinn a' snámh.

28.   " Threigeas gu h-eibhneach Uladh,
Fa 'n triuir churaidh a' b' annsadh ;
Mo shaoghal 'nan déigh chan fhada—
Na h-eagar fear ath bhuailt dhomhsa.

29.   " Tri ialla nan tri chon sin,
Do bhuin osnadh o m' chridhe ;

'S ann agamsa bhiodh an tasgaidh,—
Am faicsinn is aobhar cumhadh.

30. " A Chlann Uisnich tha an sud thall—
'N 'ur luidhe bonn re bonn ;
Da' n súmhlaicheadh mairbh roimh bheo eile,
Shúmhlaicheadh sibhse romham-sa.

31. " A thriuir threun o Dhun-monaidh,—
A thriuir ghiollan nam feart buadha ;—
Tar éis an triuir ni maireann mise, —
Triuir le 'm briseadh mo luchd fuatha.

32. " Air fosgladh am feartan,
Na déanaibh an uaigh gu docair ;—
Bitheam am fochair na h-uaighe,
Far nach deanar truaigh na ochain.

33. " An tri sgiathan 's an tri sleaghan,
Anns an leabaidh chumhainn cuiribh ;—
Cáiribh an tri chlaidhmhean cruadhach,
Sínte os cionn uaigh nam mín-fhear.

34. " An tri conaibh 's an tri seabhaic ;—
Biotar am feasd gun luchd seilge—
Cuiribh an gar nan triath chatha—
Triar dhalta Chonaill Chearnaich.

35. " Och is truagh mo shealladh orra,—
     Fáth mo dhocair as mo thúrsaidh ;—
     Nach do chuireadh mi 's an talamh,
     Sul mharbhadh geala mhac Uisnich.

36. " Is mise Dearduil gun éibhneas,
     Nis a' críochnachadh mo bheatha ;
     Bronnam, le m' chridhe, mo thri póga,
     As dùineam am brón mo láithean."

37. Shín i 'n sin a taobh r' a thaobh,
     Agus chuir i 'beul r' a bheul,
     As ghabh i 'n sgian roimh a cridhe,
     'S fhuair i 'm bás gun aithreachas ;
     Ach thilg i 'n sgian dubh 's a' chuan,
     Mu 'm faigheadh an saor achmhasan.

38. Ráinig Conchar an tráigh,
     Is cúig ceud an coinneamh a mhnaoi ;—
     'S e fhuair e 'n sin, gun agadh,
     Na ceithir cuirp sínte síos cho fhada.

CONCHAR.

39. " Míle mallachd míle mairg,
     Air a' chéill atá gam' chumail ;—
     Air a' chéill a thug ormsa
     Deagh chlann mo pheathar féin a mharbhadh.

40. " Tha iadsan gun anam dheth—
    Tha mise gun Dheardra agam ; —
    Ach tiolaicidh mi 'n aon uaigh,
    Naois as Deirdri 'n aon leabaidh ;—
    'S an lus beag a thig roimh 'n uaigh,—
    Ge b' e chuireas snaim air a bharr—
    Gum bu leis aon rogha leannain.

41. " Na 'm bithinnsa 'N Iubhar nam buaih,
    A nocht féin ga fuar an t-sian ;—
    Gun cuirinnsa snaim air a bharr—
    Ge do bhiodh an crann gu críona."

Fraoch Mac Fithich.

Auctor Hujus in Keich O Cloan.

1. H-osna charaid a Cluain Fraoich—
   H-osna laoich a caiseal chró,—
   H-osna dhéanadh túrsach fear,
   Agus d' an guilionn bean óg.

2. Aig so shear an carn fa' n bheil
   Fraoch Mac Fithich an fhuilt mhaoith ;—
   Fear a rinn buidheachas do Mhaoibh
   Is bho shlointear Carn Fraoich.

3. Gul aon mhná an Cruachan Soir,—
   Truagh an sgeul fa bheil a' bhean ;
   Is e bheir a h-osna gu trom,
   Fraoch Mac Fithich nan colg sean.

4. Is i an aon bhean do ni an gul,
   A' dul d' a éis gu Cluain Fraoich ;—
   Ainnir an fholt chas, áil—
   Inghean Mhaoibh g' a bitheadh laoich.

5. Inghean Orla is ordha folt
   Is Fraoch an nocht taobh air thaobh ;
   Ga mór fear do ghrádhaich i,—
   Nior ghrádhaich si fear ach Fraoch.

6. Faigheas Maoibh mu fuath,
   Cáirdeas Fraoich fa fear a gleoidh ;—
   A chúis fa chreuchtadh a chorp,
   Tre gun locht a dhéanamh dhith.

7. Do chuir i e gus a' bhás,
   Taobh re mnáthaibh ni tug o 'n olc ;
   Mór am púdhar a thuit le Maoibh—
   Innisead gun cheilg a nois.

8. Caorthainn do bhi air Loch Maidh,—
   Do chimid an tráigh dha dheas ;—
   Gach ráidhe—gach mí—
   Toradh abaidh do bhi air.

9. Sása bhi an caorthainn sin,—
   Fa milse na mil a bhláth ;—
   Do chongfagh a caoran dearg
   Fear gun bhiadh gu ceann naoi trátha.

10. Bliadhna air shaoghal gach fir,
    Do chuireadh sin fa sgeul dhearbh ;—
    Gum b' fhóirinn do lucht chneidh
    Frith a mheas is e dearg.

11. Do bhi ainseun 'na dhiaigh,
    Ga bith e, léigh a chobhradh an t-slóigh ;—

Péist nimh dho bhith 'na bhun,
Bh' aca dho chath dhol d' a bhuain.

12. Bhi an easláinte throm—throm,—
Inghean Athaich nan corn saor ;—
Do chuireadh leatha fios air Fraoch ;—
Fiosraich ciod tháin' rìth'.

13. A dubhairt Maoibh nach biodh slán,
Mar faigheadh lán a boise maoith,
Do chaoraibh an locha fhuair,
Gun duine dh' a bhuain ach Fraoch.

14. Cnuasachd riamh ni dhearn mi,
Ars' Mac Fithich nan gruaidh dearg
Ge geur dhearnas e air Fraoch,
Racham do bhuain chaor do Mhaoibh.

15. Gluaiseas Fraoch, fa fear an áigh,
Bhuain dho shnámh air an loch ;
Fhuair e phéist, is i 'na suain,
Is a ceann suas ris an dos.

16. Fraoch Mac Fithich, an airm ghéir,
Tháinig o 'n phéist gun fhios díth ;—
Thug e ultach chaora dearg,
Far an robh Maoibh dh' a tí.

MAOIBH.

17. " Ach ge maith na thugas leat,"
A dubhairt Maoibh is geal cruth,
" Ni fhóir mise, a laoich luinn,
Ach slat a bhuain as a bun."

18. Togras Fraoch—is nior ghille tiom—·
A shnámh a rís air an linn bhuig ;—
Is nior fheud, ach ga mór 'ágh,
Theachd o 'n bhás an robh chuid.

19. Gabhas an caorthainn air bharr—
Tarruingidh an crann as a fhreumh ;—·
Toirt dó a chos dho an tír,
Mothaigheas dho rís a' phéist.

20. Beireas air agus e air snámh,
Is gabhas a lámh 'na craos ;—
Do ghabh esan ise air ghial,—
Truagh gun a sgian aig Fraoch !

21. Ainnir, an fholt chais áil,
Do ráin' chuige le sgian do 'n ór ;
Leadair a' phéist a chneas bán
Is teasgadh a lámh air luath.

22. Do thuiteadar bonn ri bonn,
Air tráigh nan clach corr fa dheas ;

Fraoch Mac Fithich is a' phéist—
Truagh a Dhé mar thug an treis.

23. 'Ga comhrag—ni comhrag gearr,—
Do rug leis a ceann 'na laimh ;
Mar chonnaic an nighean e,
Do chuaidh 'na neul air an tráigh.

24. Eireas an nighean o 'n támh,—
Gabhas an lámh—bu lámh bhog ;

AINNIR.

" Ga ta so 'na chuid nan eun,
Is mór an t-euchd a rinn a bhos."

25. Bho 'n bhás sean do fhuair am fear,
Loch Mai go lean do 'n loch ;—
A ta an t-arm sean dith, gu luain,
'G a ghairm a nuas gus a nois.

26; Beirear, an sean, gu Cluan Fraoich,
Corp an laoich go Caiseal chróigh ;—
Air a' ghleann thugadh, a ainm,
Is mairg a mhaireas d' a luaidh.

27. Carn laimh an carn so ri m' thaobh,—
A laimh ris do bhitheas sonn ;
Fear nior iompoigheadh an treise,—
Fear bu dhásaiche neart an trod.

28. Ionmhuinn am beul nior ob dhaimh,—
    A 'm bitheadh mnathan a tobhairt phóg ;
    Ionmhuinn tighearn nan sluagh,—
    Ionmhuinn gruaidh nior dheirge 'n rós.

29. Duibhe no fitheach barr a fholt,
    Deirge a ghruaidh no fuil laoigh ;
    Fa míne na cobhar sruth,
    Gile na an sneacht, cneas Fraoich.

30. Caise na an caisein fholt,—
    Guirme a rosg na oidhre-leac ;—
    Deirge na partainn* a bheul,—
    Gile a dheud na bláth féith.

31. Airde a shleagh na crann siuil,—
    Binne no teud chiuil a ghuth ;—
    Snámhaiche do b' fhearr no Fraoch,
    Cha do shín a thaobh ri sruth.

32. Fa leithne na cómhla a sgiath,—
    Ionmhuinn trath bhith ri druim ;—
    Co fada 'lámh is a lann,—
    Leithne a cholg na clár dhe long.

     *Partaiun-dearg :—*Rowan berries*

33. Truagh nach ann an cómhrag ri laoch,
    Do thuit Fraoch a bhronnadh ór ;—
    Tursa sin a thuiteam le péist—
    Truagh, a dhé na mairionn fós.

Conlaoch.

Gille-calum Mac an Ollaimh an t-ursgeul so sios

Transliterated from Dr. Mac Lauchlan's Transcript of Dean Mac Gregor's Book.

. *Quatrains 24, 25, 26, 27, 30, and 31, are from Gillies' Collection of Gaelic Songs and Poems.*

---

1. Do chuala mi fad o shean,
   Sgeul do bhoineas ri cumha ;
   Is tráth dh' a h-aithris gu trom,
   Ga ta e mar ainnis oirnn.

2. Clanna Rughraidh nam bráth mall
   Fa Chonchobhair is fa Chonaill ;
   Do b' úrlaimh óigfhir air mhagh,
   Air h-urlar Choigeimh Uladh.

3. G' a thigh, ni tháinig, le gean,
   Fa uile laochraidh Bhanbha ;
   Cath ag faghail aon uair eile,
   Dar dh' iomain Clanna Rughraidh.

E

4.   Tháinig chugainn—borb a fhraoch—
      An curaidh crodha Conlaoch;
      A dh' fhiosnadh m' ar cláraibh grinn,
      O Dhun-Sgathaich gu h-Eirinn.

5.   Do labhair Conchobhar ri cách,
      Co gheibheamar chon an óglaich,
      Do bhreith beacht nan sgeula dheth,
      Gun teachta le h-euradh bhuaidh?

6.   Gluaiseas Conall, nior lag lámh,
      Do bhreith sgeula de 'n mhacan;
      Air dearbh tarruinn do 'n laoch,
      Ceanghailear Conall le Conlaoch.

7.   Nior ghobh an laoch le lámhach
      Chonaill fraoich forranaich;
      Ceud d' ar sluagh do cheanghladh leis—
      Ioghnadh a 's buan ri aithris!

8.   Chuireadh teachtair gu ceann nan con,
      Bho h-ard-righ eagnaidh Uladh,
      Gu Dun-dealgain ghrianach, ghloin—
      Seann dún céillidh nan Gáidheal.

9.   (Bho 'n dún sin do luadhar leinn)
      Do dh' eangnamh nighean Fhorgain;

Thigeas gniomhaidhe nan saoradh seang
Gu righ faoilteach nam fearann.

10. Dh' fhiosraicheadh sluagh Uladh uaine,—
Thigeas Cú na Craoibhe Ruaidhe ;—
Mac deud-fhionn—a ghruaidh mar shugh—
Nior eitich teacht d' ar cobhair.

CONCHOBHAR.

11. "Fada," ars' Conchobhar ris a' Chú,
"Bhathas gun teacht d' ar cobhair ;
As Conall, suireach nan steud meara,
An cuibhreach as ceuda d' ar sluagh."

CONALL.

12. "Deacair dhomhsa bhith am bruid,
A fhir a chobhradh air caraid !"

CUCHULAINN.

"Ni 'n réidh dol an eangnamh a lainne,—
Eise le r' cheanghladh Conall."

CONALL.

13. "Na smaoinich gun dol 'na aghaidh,
A righ nan gorm-lann gráineil !
A lámh chruaidh gun luige ri neach,
Smuainich air t' oide, a's e 'n cuibhreach.

14. Cuchulainn nan sean lann sliom,
    Nuair a chual e tuireadh Chonaill ;
    Do ghluais e, le tréine a lámh,
    Do bhreith sgeula de 'n mhacamh."

CUCHULAINN.

15. "Innis dhuinn, air teachd a' d' dháil,
    A Raic ! an tu nior ob teugbhail ?
    A shlios réidh an abhraidh dhuibh—
    Fios t' airm ? Co do dhuthchas ? "

CONLAOCH.

16. " Do m' gheasaibh air teacht bho m' thigh,
    Gun sgeula dh' innseadh a dh' aoidhe ;
    Da 'n innsinn do neach eile,—
    A' d' dreachsa dh' innsinn, gu h-áraid."

CUCHULAINN.

17. "Comhrag riumsa is éigin duit,
    Na sgeul a innseadh mar charaid ;
    Gabhsa do rogha, a chiabh lag ;—
    Ni céillidh tigeil a' m' chomhrag."

CONLAOCH.

18. "Ach na bhitheadh gun tigeadh 'n ar ceann !
    A h-Onnchu áidh na h-Eireann !

A lámh ghaisge an tús troid!
Mo chliú bhith an nasgaidh agad."

19. Iomaineadar chon a chéile,—
Ni ta 'n comhrag banamhail;
Am macan gun d' fhuair a ghuin—
An daltan cruaidh, lámhach.

20. Cuchulainn as comhrag cruaidh,
Do bha 'n lá sin fo dhiombuaidh;
A! aon mhac do mharbhadh leis—
An t-saor-shlat chalma, chaomh ghlas!

CUCHULAINN.

21. "Innis duinn," arsa Cú nan cleas,
O, ta am feasta fo 'r n-áilleas,
T' arm as do shloinneadh gu lom:—
Na teirig a dh' fholchainn oirnn."

CONLAOCH.

22. "Is mi Conlaoch mac a' Choin,
Oighre dligheach Dhun-dealgain:—
Is mi 'n rún dh' fhágas am broinn,
As tu aig Sgathaich ga t'fhoghlum.

23. "Seachd bliadhna do bha mi shoir,
A foghlum ghaisge bho m' mháthair;

Na cleasa le 'n do thorchair mi.
Bha dh' easbhuidh an fhoghluim orm.

24. " Thoir thusa leat mo shleagh,
Agus buain an sgiath so dhiomsa ;
'S thoir leat mo chlaidheamh cruadhach—
Lann fhuair mi air a líomhadh.

25. " Thoir mo mhallachd gu m' mháthair,
O 's i cháirich mi fo gheasaibh ;
'S a chuir an láthair m' fhuluing,—
A Chuchulainn—b' ann le d' chleasaibh.

26. A Chuchulainn chaoimh, chrios-ghil,
Leis am brisear gach bearn ghàbhaidh ;
Nach amhairc thu—as mi gun aithne—
Cia meur mu 'm bheil am fáine.

27. " Is olc a thuigeadh tusa uamsa,
Athair uasail, ana-méinich ;
Gur *mi* thilgeadh, gu fann, fiar—
An t-sleagh an coinneamh a h-earlainn !"

28. Smaoineas Cuchulainn nuair a dh' eug,
A mhac an dreach do chumhadh ;
Gur smaoin, nar bhréig, faoilte an fhir,—
Do thréig a chuimhne 's a cheudfadh.

29. A airmidh, ri corp a' Choin,
   A chumha 's beag nach do sgar,
   Ri faicinn, an culthaobh a' ghlinne,
   Gaisgeach Dhuine-dealgain.

CUCHULAINN.

30. " Na mairinns' as Conlaoch slán,
   Ag iomairt air chleasa an comhlan ;
   Chuireamaid cath formadach, treun,
   Air fearaibh Alba agus Eireann.

31. " Dh' iath umam ceud cumha,
   Mi bhith dubhach ni h-ioghnadh ;
   O m' chomhrag ri m' aon mhac,
   Mo chreuchdan a nochd is iomadh."

GLOSSARY

TO THE PRECEDING

Gaelic Ballads.

Contractions used in Glossary.

Adj. Adjective; *adv.* Adverb; *s.* Substantive; *sg.* Singular; *pl.* Plural; *s. m.* Substantive masculine; *s. f.* Substantive feminine; *sg. gen.* Singular genitive; *sg. dat.* Singular dative; *pl. nom.* Plural nominative; *pl dat.* Plural dative; *pl gen.* Plural genitive; *asp.* Aspirated. The acute accent is placed over long vowels.

GLOSSARY.

A

Abaidh, *adj. ripe.* Adhart, *s. m. a bolster, a pillow.* Aidhe, *sg. gen. of* Adh, *s. f. a heifer.* Ailde, *adj. more or most handsome, or comely.* Aille, *s. f. beauty, handsomeness, comeliness.* Aille, *adj. more or most beautiful, handsome, or comely.* Aingeis, *s. f. malice.* Ainseun, *s. f. misfortune, mischance, mishap.* Ail, *adj. modest, beautiful, noble.* Aillead, *s. f. beauty, handsomeness.* Aiteal, *s. m. a short portion of time.* Aisnichean, *s. f. pl. ribs.* Aisling, *s. f. a dream.* Aithris, *s. f. recital, rehearsal, report, narration.* Aluinn, *adj. fair, beautiful, handsome, comely.* Amhas, *s. m. an ungovernable man; a soldier.* Allmharach, *s. m. a foreigner; a barbarian.* Aonach, *s. m. a hill, a steep height, heath, height, desert place.* Aonaran, *s. m. a recluse, a hermit, one who lives alone.* Athchuinge, *s. f. a prayer, a request.*

B

Bárr, *s. m. top or extremity.* Bas-tana, *adj. thin-hoofed.* Beag-ghaoisdneach, *adj. small-haired.* Binn, *adj. melodious, sweet, true.* Bian, *s.m. a skin or a hide.* Beireas, *imp. verb, catches.* Boise, *sg. gen. of* bos *or* bas, *the open hand.* Bonn, *s. m. a sole; a foundation; a bottom or base; a coin; a bit, the smallest part.* Bior-chul-chas, *s. m. a pin holding together the hind legs of a cow or bullock killed, and hung up to dry.* Bládh, *s. m. renown, fame.* Beum, *s. a blow, a hurt.* Bailg-fhionn, *adj. white-bellied.* Braonach, *adj. rainy; sorrowful.* Braon-sgeul, *s. m. a sorrowful story.* Bréagh, *adj. comely, handsome.* Brigh *or* brí, *s. a word.* Bráigh, *s. m. a hostage, a captive, a prisoner; pl.* Bráighde *and* braighdean. Brath, *s. m. information.* Bráth, *s. m. judgment.* Bruan, *s. m. a splinter.* Beart, *s. a manner of doing a thing; dress, clothing; s. f. an action, a deed.* Bláth, *s. m. a flower, a blossom.* Buidhne, *sg. gen. of* Buidheann *s. f., a band.* Baighe, *s. a fight, a combat, a battle.* Bronnadh, *s. giving, bestowing, a gift.* Bronnaim, *v. I give, bestow.* Brághad, *s. m. the neck, throat, windpipe.* Bradan, *s. m. a salmon.* Bhroinne, *asp. pl. gen. of* Brú, *s. f. a belly.* Bruthaichean, *pl. nom. of s. m.* bruthach, *an acclivity or a declivity; a brae.* Buideachas, *s. thanks, gratitude; kindness.* Buadha, *sg.*

gen. of buaidh, *s. f. victory, conquest; virtue, power.*
Buadhach, *adj. victorious; estimable, valuable, precious.*
Bhuainn, *from us.* Briseadh, *s. a breaking, a battle,*
a conquest.

C

Caogad, *adj. fifty.* Caladh, *s. m. a harbour, a haven,*
a port. Caol, *adj. slender, fine, small.* Caolchasach,
adj. slender-legged. Cathair, *s. f. a fort, a city.* Cearnach, *adj. victorious.* Cearn, *s. m. a victory.* Ceathach,
s. m. mist, fog, vapour. Céin, *adj. far, remote.* Clisniche,
sg. gen. of clisneach, *s. m. the human body; a carcase.?*
Cli, *s. the body.* Cliar, *s. m. a troop.* Chinnfhionn, *asp.*
form of adj. ceann-fhionn, *white-headed.* Caomh, *adj.*
handsome, comely. Ceannardach, *adj. proud, imperious.*
Ceard, *s. m. a smith, a tinker.* Carraig, *s. f. a rock.*
Cailg-fhionn, *adj. white haired or white-bristled.* Chon-
airc, *v. saw.* Cobhair, *s. f. help, aid, succour.* Cath,
s. m. a battle; a battalion. Comhradh, *s. m. talk,*
conversation, discourse. Comhrag, *s. m. a combat, a*
conflict. Cleas, *s. m. a feat, a dexterous deed.* Cliabh-
fharsuinn, *adj. wide-chested.* Craobhach, *adj. arboreous.*
Cluanach, *adj. belonging to a meadow or plain.* Cnámh-
ach, *adj. bony.* Cleachdach, *adj. having clustering*
ringlets or tresses. Cleachd, *s. f. a ringlet of hair.*
Cluas-bheag, *adj. small eared.* Céire, *sg. gen. of* céir

s. f. wax. Cagar, *s. m. a whisper, a secret.* Coimhiche, *sg. gen. of s. m.* coimheach, *a stranger.* Colann, *s. f. the body.* Claoin, *for* cluain, *s. f. a plain, a lawn; a retired situation.* Chitheam, *v. I see.* Cruinneagach, *adj. low and round with respect to a woman.* Ciomach, *s. m. a captive or a prisoner.* Coinneamh, *s. f. a meeting.* Cuibhreachadh, *s. m. a binding, a fettering.* Cumha, *s. m. lamentation, sorrow.* Corn, *s. m. a drinking horn or cup.* Clocharra, *adj. set with stones.* Cos, *s. f. foot and leg., pl. gen* cos. Conchar, *contr. of* Conchobhar *or* Conchobhor. Clochaibh, *pl. dat. of* cloch, *s. f. a stone.* Cruaidh, *adj. hard.* Colg, *s. m. a sword; rage, wrath.* Chimid, *v. we see.* Caoir-theine, *s. f. a fire brand; sparkling flame.* Creuchta, *adj. wounded.* Cumaiseach, *for adj.* cumasach *strong, powerful.* Croidh-fhionn, *adj. white-hoofed.* Cuirp, *sg. gen. and pl. nom. of* corp, *s. m. a body.* Cú, *s. m. a king, a champion.* Cuan, *s. m. a bay, a haven; an ocean.* Cumhachdach, *adj. mighty, powerful.* Coimh-reidh, *adj. even, level.* Conaibh, *pl. dat. of* Cú, *s. m. a hound or dog; used for the pl. nom.* Cothrom, *s. m. equity, justice; an advantage.* Cuallach, *s. f. company.* Curaidh, *s. m. a champion.* Caorthainn, *s. mountain ash, rowan tree.* Alb. Caorrunn. *s. m. mountain ash or rowan tree.* Craos, *s. m. a wide mouth.* Corr, *adj. round.* [This word forms part of three place-names in Islay:—Corra-bheinn, *round-mountain.* Loch Corr, *round lake, and* Cnocan corr, *round knoll.*] Cnuasachd, *s. f. wild fruit gathering.*

D

Dáimh, *s. m. and f. relationship, friendship.* Dalta, *s. m. a foster child; dim.* daltan. Dáil, *s. f. a meeting.* Dán, *s. m. fate, destiny.* Deagh-mhaiseach, *adj. excellently, beautiful.* Dearg, *adj. red.* Deimhin, *adj. certain, sure, true.* Dearsa-fhionn, *adj. bright-shining.* Dearmad, *s. m. omission.* Dásach, *adj. fierce, bold.* Deiream, *I say.* Deórachd, *s. f. banishment, exile.* Dil, *adj. fond, faithful.* Díonadh, *s. m. a defending.* Diongmhail *for* Diongadh, *s. m. act of matching, overcoming, conquering.* Deud, *s. m. a tooth; the jaw; set of teeth.* Doinionn, *s. f. inclement weather; storm, tempest.* Domhain, *sg. gen. of* Domhan, *s. m. the world.* Dorsair, *s. m. a porter, a doorkeeper.* Do dh', *contraction of* do dho, *a reduplication.* Dú, *fit, proper, (i. dual. O' Clery.)* Dubhairt, *v. said.* Duileadh, *adj. sadder.* Dún, *s. m. a fort.* Dual, *s. m. a loop, a fold, a plait.* Dual, *for* Dualadh, *s. m. the act of carving, a piece of carved work.* Drithleann, *s. m. a sparkle.*

E

Ealla, *adv. nothing ado.* Eangach, *adj. nailed, hooked.* Eachmhor, *adj. horse—large.* Eagnuidhe, *adj.*

expert, judicious. Earrann, *s. f. a sharp pain in the side; a stitch.* Ealchainn, *s. f. a stand for arms.* Eidhre, *s. f. ice.* Eilde, *sg. gen. of* Eilid, *s. f. a hind.* Eineach, *s. m. courtesy; generosity.* Eis, *s. f. delay, detention, hindrance.* Eirig, *s. f. a ransom, a forfeit, a fine; reparation, amercement.* Eitidh, *adi. boisterous, fierce, dreadful, ugly.*

F

Faiche, *s. f. a field, a plain.* Famhair, *s. m. a giant.* Fann, *adj. weak.* Faonach *for* Aonach, *s. m. a hill, a steep; height, heath, desert place.* Faoibh, *s. f. a relic; dead men's clothes.* Faoil, *s. f. hospitality, generosity.* Faoil, *s. m. patience, forbearance.* Faoil, *adj. wild, untameable.* Faol, Fulang, *patience.* Farum, *s. m. rustling noise.* Fáth, *s. m. cause, reason; opportunity.* Faircill, *s. pl. instruments for holding the hair properly.* Feall-sgáth, *s. m. false fear, cowardice.* Feall, *s. m. treachery, falsehood, deceit.* Fearaibh, *dat. pl. of* Fear. Fear, *s. m. a man, a male.* Fairich, *v. to perceive.* Feart, *s. m. a virtue; a grave.* Flath, *s. m. a lord, a hero.* Fail, *s. f. a ring.* Fáine, *s. f. and m. a ring.* Fial, *adj. good.* Fianuis, *s. f. a witness; evidence, testimony.* Faoidh. *s. departing; a voice, a sound; sleep.* Fionda, *adj. cerulean. sky-coloured.* Fionn, *adj. white, fair.* Fioghurdha, *decorated with emblematical figures.* Fionn-bhuidhe, *adj. light yellow.* Fóir, *s. f. help, relief.* Foighneachd, *s. f. an inquiring, an asking, a questioning.* Fóirinn, *s. f. aid, help, remedy.* Frith, *s. f. profit, gain, advantage, benefit.* Fhuilt, *asp. sg. gen. of* Folt, *s. m. the hair of the head.* Fuath, *s. m. hatred, aversion, abhorrence.*

G

Gall, *s. m. a pillar stone, or boundary stone; dim.* Gallan, *means the same.* Gall, *s. m., now denotes, in the Scottish Highlands, the Scottish Lowlanders, and in Ireland, the Irish who do not speak Gaelic.* It would seem to be the word Gall, a boundary stone with the extended meaning of one outside the boundary of the Gael. Gallan, *dim. of* Gall, *also a boundary stone, or standing stone.* These words enter into place-names in Ireland. Cangallia is the name of a place near Castle-island in the county of Kerry, which is, in Gaelic, *Ceann-gaille*, head of standing stone. Several places named Gallagh, derived from *gallach*, abounding in standing stones, or large stones or rocks, are found in all the provinces of Ireland, excepting Munster. A parish in Meath is called Gallow, a name, also, derived from *Gallach.* Gallan, *s. m. a branch, a sapling; a youth.* Gabhas, *v. takes.* Geal, *white, clear.* Geall, *s. m. a pledge, mortgage.* Géill, *s. f. yielding, submission.* Giollan, *pl. nom. of* Giolla, *s. m. a lad, a youth.* Giollan,

F

dim. of Giolla; *a young lad.* Goith, *pl. gen. of* Goth, *s. m. a spear.* Gnúis, *s. f. the face, countenance.* Gorm, *adj. blue; red.* Geug, *s. f. a branch.* Gial, *s. f. a jaw, a cheek.* Gleóidh, *sg. gen. of* Gleódh, *s. m. a sigh, a groan.* Grinn, *adj. fine, elegent, beautiful.* Grinnghruagach, *adj. fine-haired.* Guin, *s. m. pain; a wound, a dart, a sharp point; fierceness.* Guin, *v. wound. pierce, sting.* Gurt, *s. m. pain, fierceness.* Goire, *adj. contiguous.* Gul, *s. m. weeping, lamentation.* Guilionn, *v. would lament or weep.*

I

Iath *or* Iadh, *v. to surround or encompass.* Iath, *s. land, country.* Iomad, *adj. many.* Iomarbhaidh, *s. m. strife, contention.* Iomarsgal, *s. wrestling.* Inghean, *s. f. a daughter, a maiden, a virgin.* Innisead, *v. let me tell.* Ialla, *s. thongs.* Iolaire, *sg. gen. of* Iolar, *s. m. an eagle.* Ionmhas, *s. m. treasure.*

L

Láidir, *adj. strong.* Lainnire *for* Lainnreach, *adj. effulgent, radiant, glossy.* Lachaibh, *pl. dat. of* Lacha, *s. a duck or drake.* Laoigh, *sg. gen. and pl. nom. of* Laogh, *s. m. a calf.* Leachdainn, *sg. dat. of* Leachdann, *s. f. the side of a hill; steep, shelving ground; used for* Leaca, *s. f. the cheek.* Leug, *s. f. a gem.* Leadair, *v. tran. mangled.* Lán-ghlic, *adj. thoroughly wise.*

Learg, *s. m. a little eminence, a plain, a beaten path, a
sea coast, a beach.* Liath, *adj. grey, hoary.* Líobharra,
adj. polished. Líomharra, *adj. polished, burnished.*
Loinnearra, *adj. bright, shining.* Luathmhor, *adj. most
swift, most fleet.* Linn, *s. f. a lake.* Lúghmhor, *adj.
vigorous, very strong.* Laoch, *a warrior.* Leachd, *s.
f. a bed.* Loingeas *or* Luingeas, *s. f. shipping, a fleet.*
Luinn, *sg. voc. of adj,* Lonn, *strong, brave.* Lúthmhor,
adj, agile, nimble.

M

Magh, *s. m. and f. a plain, a field.* Macanachd, *s.
ordering, directing.* Maigheach, *s. f. a hare.* Maith,
s. m. a chief, a noble. Maoigh *for* Múigh, *sg. dat. of*
Magh. Mac-samhailt, *s. m. emblem or resemblance.*
Maireann, *adj. living.* Maoisleach, *s. f. a hind.*
Maorach, *s. m. all kinds of shell-fish.* Marascal, *s. m.
a master.* Mall, *adj. slow.* Mathghamhna, *sg. gen.,
and nom. pl. of* Mathghamhainn, *a bear.* Mnath-
aibh, *pl. dat. of bean, a woman.* Mnathan, *pl. nom. of*
bean. Mhna, *asp. sg. gen. of* bean. Mearganta, *adj.
brisk, lively, sportive.* Meangan, *s. m. a branch, a twig,
a bough.* Meur, *s. m. and f. a finger; a branch or a
bough.* Mothaid, *adj. greater.* Míorun, *s. m. malice,
spite, malevolence.* Miann, *s. m. and f. desire, will, wish,
inclination.* Muadh, *adj. noble, good.* Gu muadh, *adv.*

well. Meamnach, *cheerful, high-spirited, courageous, magnanimous.* Mugh, *v. to change.* Mór-chuinnein-each, *adj. large-nostriled.* Meoir, *sg. gen. and nom. pl of* meur, *a finger.* Mí, *s. f. a month.* Muineal, *s. m. the neck.* Múirneach, *adj. cheerful, joyful, affectionate.*

N

Na cantair *for* Na can, *v. speak not.* Ni faighim, *v. I am not able to obtain.* Néarachd, *s. a happy or lucky person.* Nimh, *sg. dat. of s. f.* Neimh, *poison.* Neónach, *adj. strange, curious, wonderful.* Nior, a compound of the negative, adverb *ni,* and *ro,* a particle like *do,* preceding the past tense of verbs. Nunn, *adv. over* Null, *adv. over.* Nior ob, *v. did not refuse.* Nois, *adv. now.*

O

Omar, *s. m. amber.* Oglach, *s. m. a youth, a servant, a vassal, a soldier, a kern.* Orbhuidhe, *adj. gold yellow.* Oidhre, *s. f. ice.* Oir, *adj. east.* Orruidh, *adj. golden-coloured.* Ordha, *gold-coloured.* Os, *above.* Osna, *s. f. a sigh.* Ospartaich, *s. panting.*

P

Péist, *s. f. a worm, a beast, a monster; a serpent.* Port, *s. m. a fort, a stronghold; a port, a harbour.* Prap, *adj. quick.* Pronnadh, *s. pounding, bruising, or mincing.* Púdhar, *s. m. hurt, harm, damage.*

R

Rachainn, *v. I go.* Rag, *adj. stiff, rigid, pertinacious, inflexible.* Rosg, *s. m. an eye.* Rádharc *or* Fradharc, *s. m. sight, sense of seeing.* Randa, *adj. true, sincere, faithful.* Reamhar, *adj. fat.* Raoir, *adv. last night.* Rogha, *s. m. choice.* Ráidhe, *s. m. a quarter of the year.* Ráin, *contr. of v.* Rainig, *reached.*

S

Sáile, *s. m. salt-water.* Sálta, *pl. nom. of s. f.* sál, *a heel.* Sealbh, *s. f. a herd; possession, inheritance.* Seang, *adj. slender, slender-waisted; stately.* Sál, *s. m. salt-water.* Seabhac, *s. m. a hawk, a falcon.* Saoth-raiche, *s. m. a persistent worker.* Seudaidh, *adj. jewelled.* Sealladh, *s. m. sight, eyesight, power of vision,* Sean, Seann, *adj. old, ancient.* Salach, *adj. dirty.* Seiche, *s. f. a hide or skin.* Sgáin, *v. to burst.* Searbh, *adj. bitter.* Sgeir, *s. f. a skerry.* Spéis, *s. f. regard, attachment, fondness.* Searrachail, *adj. foal-like.* Sliom, *adj. slim, sleek.* Sean, *adj. that.* An sean. *adv. there.* Slán, *adj. whole, healthy.* Saoghal, *s. m. the world; life; an age, a generation.* Sgar, *v. to scatter or separate.* Scar, *adj. east.* Shear, *asp. form of* sear. Sreunaibh *for* Srianaibh, *pl. dat. of s. f.* srian, *a bridle.* Sín, *v. to stretch.* Sochd, *s. silence.* Socht, *s. m. silence, quiet.* Soir, *adj. east.* Suain, *sg. dat. of* Suan, *s. m. sleep, deep sleep.* Sleamhuinn, *adj. smooth.* Sról-bhreideach, *adj. satin-bannered.* Sróll, *s. m. satin.* Shlointear, *v. is named.* Slointear leat, *v. they shall be named by thee.* Slios-tana, *adj. thin flanked.* Sluagh, *s. m. a host, an army, a multitude; people.* Sparradh, *s. m. act of driving or thrusting.* Sonn, *s. m. a prince, a hero, sg. gen. and pl. nom.* Suinn. Sgleó *for* gleó, *s. m. a fight, an uproar, a tumult, a disturbance.* Sruth, *s. m. a stream, a current.* Stuthmhor, *adj. mettlesome.* Steudmhor, *adj. steed—large.* Sgrios, *s. f. ruin, destruction, devastation, wreck.* Suiridh, *s. f. courting, wooing.* Slios, *s. m. a side; a long sloping declivity.* Stuadhmhor, *adj. as applied to horses, large-chested.* Steudmhor, *adj. steed—large.* Snoigheadh, *s. chipping, hewing.* Suairc, *adj. pleasant, facetious, agreeable.* Snuadh, *s. colour, hue, appearance.* Sleagh, *s. f. a spear, a pike, a lance.* Súrd, *s. m. alacrity, eager, exertion, industry, speed.*

T

Támh, *s. m. a swoon.* Táintean, *pl. nom. of s. f.* Táin; *herds; spoils; mental endowments.* Táth, *adj. firm, compact.* Teinn, *s. f. distress.* Tí, *s. design, intention.* Teamhra, *sg. gen. of* Teamhair, *a place from which a prospect is commanded.* Teamhair, *s. f, Tara,*

in Meath, the seat of the ancient Irish monarchs.
Teamhair, *s. f. a covered or shaded walk upon a hill for
a convenient prospect.* Teamhair, *adj. pleasant, agreeable.* Targaideach, *adj. shielded.* Tláth, *adj. smooth,
soft.* Tiúbhradh, *v. would give.* Teud chiúil, *s. f. a
music string.* Tighearn, *s. m. a lord.* Togadar, *v.
raised or lifted.* Toradh, *s. m. fruit.* Taghmhor,
adj. most choice. Tointe, *pl. nom. of* Tonn, *s. m. a skin.*
Tlachd, *s. f. pleasure, delight, gratification.* Tráth, *s.
m. time, hour; a meal.* Treun, *adj. strong, brave.*
Triar, *s. three persons.* Triall, *s. m. journeying, going,
departing.* Triath, *s. m. a king, a lord.* Trilis *or*
Trillis. *s. f. bushy hair.* Thorchair, *v. they fell or were
killed.* Trod, *s. m. strife, fight.* Truaghas, *s. m. compassion.* Tuar, *s. m. a house.* Túr, *s. m. a tower.*
Túrsach, *adj. mournful, sorrowful.* Tuinn, *sg. dat. of*
tonn, *s. m. a wave.*

U

Uamha, *sg. gen. of* Uamh, *a cave.* Uaibhreach, *adj.
haughty, proud.* Udlaidh, *adj. morose, boorish; dark,
gloomy.* Ur, *adj. perfect, faultless, comely, beautiful,
fresh.* Ultach, *s. m. a burden; an armful, a lapful.*

Ultonian Ballads.

ULTONIAN BALLADS.

Ballad of the Garve Son of Starn.

PORTER.

1. "Arise O Chief of Tara!—
I see a fleet hard to tell of!—
The bays brimful and crowded,
With the large fleet of the foreigners."

CONNELL.

2. "Thou liest, porter, greatly,—
Thou liest to-day and always;—
It is the great fleet of the plains,—
And coming to us, to aid us."

PORTER.

3. " There is a warrior at the gate of Tara—
   At the King's door, much elated ;
   Says he can take without trouble,
   And force a pledge from the men of Erin."

4. " Let me to him," said Cu-roi,—
   Also, and O' Conachar,
   Fear-dian of white side,
   And good Fraoch Son of Fiaghaidh,
   Aodh Son of Garadh of the white knee,
   And very white Cailty, Son of Ronan.

PORTER.

5. " Talk not of that, O Cu-roi,—
   Utter not discourse without strength ;—
   He shall not be fought without a ring
   Round the High Kingdom of Erin."

6. I have seen fifteen battles
   Of giants—and it's not a lie ;
   Seizing the Garve in East-land,
   In Moy-gallan of combats."

7. Then, when said Victorious Connel,—
   The lawn of Tara's battle hero ;

" I'll not engage him to my hurt ;
For in feats I am not skilful."

8.   Then when Mave said, over, within,—
Daughter of Ochy, lord of the Faynians ;—
" Let not the youth of battles in,
Into Tara house of royal heroes."

9.   Then when Connel justly said,—
The noble, comely son of Ederskol ;
O woman ! it shall not be said,
That we will refuse one man.

10.   Then was let in the big man,
Quickly, in presence of the host ;
And the place of three hundred within,
Was prepared for him that hour.

11.   Cuchullin then raised his shield,
Over the grey-topped hill ;
Nais looked on his two spears,
And Connel seized his sword.

12.   They brought in, then, the portion
Of a hundred, of food and drink, unstinted,
To be eaten, to the big man,
Who had come from the Esraidh.

13.   When satiated was the big man,
      And spent a space at drink ;
      He glanced, over from him,
      On fifty kings' sons round him.

14.   Then, when Bricten said, so well,—
      Son of Son of Cairbri from the Red Branch ;
      " Manhood and welcome to thee, without guile,
      In presence of the men of Erin."

CONNEL.

15.   " The directing of all Erin to thee, at this time,
      O Yellow-haired Bricten ;
      So long as I shall be strongly king
      Of the High Kingdom of Erin."

BRICTEN.

16.   " I would inform thee of the captives,
      With whom thou shouldst get plunder ;—
      Thine ! were Lugha Son of Cu-ree
      And Fiavy Son of Gorry.

17.   Fear-dian of white side,
      And good Fraoch Son of Fewy ;
      Aodh Son of Garra of the white knee,
      And very white Cailty, Son of Ronan.

18. " Luagha, shield of argument in renown,—
Noble son of King of Laighean Luby ;
Cormac of the fleet, so good,
Son of Son of Cairbri of the Red Branch.

19, " Fierce Bunny, who is not fierce within,
Take with thee fast from Fergu."

20. Then were taken the kings' sons,
In Tara house, in truth ;
And they were put outside,
To the brave man—in his presence.

GARVE.

21. " I do give a king's word,
Comely men of Erin ;
That I myself won't go into my ship
Without Cuchullin's submission."

CUCHULLIN.

22. " I do give the word of another king,—
'Tis what spoke the armed High Chief ;—
That thou shalt not take my submission on sea,
And I myself in life.

23. " Thou art a churl that wouldst be gloomy,—
Thou art bad thyself, and bad, thy people,—

Very bad is thy housewife,
And not better her kinsfolk;
And my submission, thou shalt not take on
And thou thyself art but a savage!"　[brine,—

24.　Then when arose the two kings,
　　With strength of swords and shields;
　　The compact earth was raised,
　　By their feet, in that hour.

25.　Many were the blows beneath rims of shields,
　　And the sounds of bodies with troops;
　　The sound of swords in the glen wind,—
　　Under the heroes' fight so tight.

26.　Seven nights and seven days,
　　They passed, in many fights;—
　　At the end of the seventh day
　　The Garve was not higher on the plain
　　Than Cuchullin in valour.

27.　At the end of the seventh day,
　　Cuchullin gave him a blow;—
　　He cleft, from splinters to chaff,
　　The nailed, gold-yellow shield.

GARVE.

28.   O, Cuchullin, know a king ;—
      My shield does not remain to me ;
      But one step of flight, east or west,
      I never took, and living.

CUCHULLIN.

29.   " I do give another king's word,"—
      'Tis what spoke the High Chief of contest ;
      " One step of flight, west or east,
      Is not in thy choice to take."

30.   Cuchullin threw, from him, his shield,
      On the field, east and west,—
      Though such was generous, bad was it's aid,
      Thought the high nobles of Erin.

31.   But Cuchullin gave another blow,
      With the greatness of his prowess and quickness;
      He raised the hand with the sword,
      And severed the head from the body.

CONNEL.

32.   " The directing of all Erin,
      To thee from me ", said Connel ;
      " And the first cup, without guile,
      In presence of the men of Erin."

G

CUCHULLIN.

33.   "I have done a deed on the Lad of the Seas!—
     Let the king believe, as is due ;—
     There is the bed of one warrior, here, who was
          on sea,
     Whose host cannot now take him away."
     Who went to Tara's house of princes,
     To force submission from the men of Erin."

Lay of the Heads.

The author of this is CONNEL, the victorious,
Son of Eddirschol.

EMER.

1. " O, Connel !—the heads are not wealth ;—
    For certain, reddened are thy arms ;—
    The heads that I see on the withe,—
    Name the men, as clad when slain."

CONNEL.

2. " Daughter of Forgall of the steeds—
    O ! young Emer of the sweet words ;
    'Tis in vengeance of Cú of feats,
    That I took with me, here, the heads."

EMER.

3. " Which is the shaggy, black, large head ?
    Redder than the rose his clear cheek ;
    It is nearest to the left side—
    That one head which has not changed hue."

CONNEL.

4. " The king of Meath's head of fleet steeds,"
    Said the son of Cairbre of bent spears ;
    " In vengeance for my own dear foster son,
    I took with me, from afar, his head."

EMER.

5. " Which is yon head, over, to my face,
    With weak, soft, and sleek hair ;
    Eye like ice, teeth like bloom,—
    Finer than all forms, his head ? "

CONNEL.

6. " Manna—he was the man of steeds,—
    The young son of Aifa who would sack every
    I left his body without head,   [bay ;
    And by me, fell all his host."

EMER.

7. " Which is this head thou takst in thy hand,
    O ! great Connel, of love to us ;
    Since Cú of the feats does not live,
    What wouldst thou give for his head's sake ?"

CONNEL.

8. " The head of Fergus' Son, of the horses,—
    Ardent in every fighting field ;—
    My sister's son of the slender tower,
    ·   I have severed from his body, his head."

EMER.

9. " Which is yon head, east, of the fair hair,
    That whips the heads to hand ?

Acquaintance I have got of his voice,—
I was, for a while, his friend."

CONNEL.

10. " Down, yonder, the Cú fell—
His body gave way with a fine form ;—
Cú son of Cú king of the Lays,—
I, after, took with me his head."

EMER.

11. " Which are these two heads, further out ?
O ! Great Connel of judgment sweet ;—
In love of thy friendship, from us don't conceal,
The names of the men wounded by thy arms."

CONNEL.

12. " The head of Leary and Clar Cuilt—
The two heads that fell by my wounds ;
Those wounded Cuchullin of victories,—
Heroes, in whose blood, I reddened my weapons."

EMER,

13. " Which are these two heads, furthest east ?
O ! Great Connel of bright deeds !
Alike, the hair's colour of the men,—
Redder their cheeks than calf's blood."

CONNEL.

14. " Good-looking Cullain and hardy Cunnlaid,
Two who were wont to prevail with wrath ;

O ! Emer—yonder east—their heads,—
I 've left their bodies in a red pool."

EMER.

15. " Which are these six heads, of bad mien,
That I do see, to my face, north ;—
Blue their faces—black their hair,
From which hardy Connel's eye turns ? "

CONNEL.

16. " Six enemies of the Cú,—
Sons of Catlidin—wonted victors !—
Those are the six warriors
Who fell by me—their arms in my hand."

EMER.

17. " O great Connel—king's father !
Which is yon head to which fight would yield ;
Gold-yellow is bushy hair from the head,
With a smooth covering, highly wrought ? "

CONNEL.

18. "Head of Son of Finn, Son of Red-haired Ros,
Son of Nic Cnee, who died by my strength ;
O ! Emer—he was the Prime !—
Leinsters's high king of speckled swords!"

EMER.

19. " O, great Connel, change the tale,—
How many fell by thy faultless hand,
Of the lamented host who are there,
In vengeance of the Cú's head ? "

CONNEL.

20. " Ten and seven scores of hundreds—
I do say is the number of men ;
Who fell by me, back on back,
By the venom of my stiff modest sword."

EMER.

21. " O, Connel,—how are they—
The women of the Inis-fáil after the Cú ?
A similar grief have they,—
Or have they no relief? "

CONNEL.

22. " O, Emer, what shall I do,
Without my Cú's assent in the silence ?
Without my dear foster son of good form,
Going from me to destruction to-night. ? "

EMER.

23. " O, Connel lift me to the grave,—
Raise my grave over the grave of the Cú ;—

In grief for him I go to death,—
Put my lips to the lips of the Cú.

24.   " I am Emer of finest form,—
Bitter vengeance I could not find ;—
To shed a tear I do not esteem,—
Woful is my stay after the Cú."

Cucbullin in bis Cbariot.

" What is the cause of thy journey or thy story ? "
" The cause of my jouney and my story
The men of Erin, yonder, as we see them,
Coming towards you on the plain.
 The Chariot on which is the fold, figured and cerulean,
Which is made strongly, handy, solid ;
Where were active, and where were vigorous ;
And where were full-wise, the noble hearted folk ;
In the prolific, faithful city ;—
Fine, hard, stone-bedecked, well-shafted ;—
Four large-chested horses in that splendid chariot ;
Comely, frolicsome.
 What do we see in that chariot ?
The white-bellied, white-haired, small-eared,
Thin-sided, thin-hoofed, horse-large, steed-large horses;
With fine, shining, polished bridles ;
Like a gem ; or like red sparkling fire ;—
Like the motion of a fawn, wounded ;
Like the rustling of a loud wind in winter ;—
Coming to you in that chariot.—
 What do we see in that chariot ?
 We see in that chariot,
The strong, broad-chested, nimble, gray horses,—
So mighty, so broad-chested, so fleet, so choice ;—

Which would wrench the sea skerries from their rocks.—
The lively, shielded, powerful horses ;—
So mett'esome, so active, so clear-shining ;—
Like the talon of an eagle 'gainst a fierce beast ;
Which are called the beautiful Large-gray—
The fond, large *Meactroigh.*

What do we see in that chariot ?—

We see, in that chariot,
The horses ; which are white-headed, white hoofed,
Fine-haired, sturdy, imperious ;   [slender-legged,
Satin-bannered, wide-chested ;
Small-aged, small-haired small-eared ;
Large-hearted, large-shaped, large-nostriled ;
Slender-waisted, long-bodied,—and they are foal-like ;
Handsome, playful, brilliant, wild-leaping ;
Which are called the *Dubh-seimhlinn.*—

Who sits in that chariot ?

He who sits in that chariot,
Is the warrior, able, powerful, well-worded,
Polished, brilliant, very graceful.—
There are seven sights on his eye ;
And we think that that is good vision to him ;
There are six bony, fat fingers,
On each hand which comes from his shoulder ;
There are seven kinds of fair hair on his head ;—

Brown hair next his head's skin,
And smooth red hair over that ;
And fair-yellow hair, of the colour of gold ;
And clasps on the top, holding it fast ;—
Whose name is Cuchullin, son *Seimh-suailte*,
Son of Aodh, son of Agh, son of other Aodh.—
His face is like red sparkles ;—
Fast-moving on the plain like mountain fleet mist ;
Or like the speed of a hill hind ;
Or like a hare on rented level ground.—
It was a frequent step—a fast step—a joyful step ;—
The horses coming towards us ;—
Like snow hewing the slopes ;—
The panting and the snorting,
Of the horses coming towards thee."

Deirdri.

1. A time that they went on the wave,—
    The Children of Uisneachan to Black Lochlann;
    They left Deirdri and the Black Lad,
    In Beinn Aird, solitary.

2. Where was heard a sadder story,
    Than the Black Lad strongly courting,
    Fair, well-shaped Deirdri?

    ### BLACK LAD.

    " It were becoming to us, to be united."

    ### DEIRDRI.

3. " Not becoming was it to me or thee,"—
    Black Lad of wicked thoughts
    But till they come home hale—
    The Children of Uisneachan from Black Lochlann."

BLACK LAD.

4. " Though death were to take thee off,
And wert thou to die without lament ;
Thou and Black John shall be in one bed,
Till earth go over thy cheek.

5. " Thou shouldst get brisk Deirdri,
From me, to-morrow morning,—
Thou shouldst get the milk of the horned cattle,
And shellfish from *Inis-aonaich.*

6. " Thou shouldst get necks of swine,
And, also, *sruthaga* of old boar ;
Thou shouldst get *braoideach* and cow,—
And O fine calf, do not suffer here."

DEIRDRI.

7. " Were I to get, from thee, the fine parts of deer,
And white-bellied salmon ;
I would like better an ox heel pin,
From the hand of Nais son of Uisneachan.—

8 " It was Nais that would kiss my lips,—
My first man and my first sweetheart,—
It was Ailly that would pour out my drink,—
And it was Ardan that would lay my pillow."

9.   But airy Deirdri looked from her,
     Out, over the top of the mournful dwelling ;—

DEIRDRI.

"Comely, the three brothers I see,—
They will swim the seas, across.

10. "Ard and Ailly at the helm,—
     Sailing, at ease, with high oars ;
     My love the white—white-handed !—
     My own man is steering you.

11. " But let no word escape thy mouth,
     Black Lad of mournful tales ;
     Lest thou be slain without guilt,—
     And neither shall I be believed.

12. " Oh, Children of Uisneachan of horses,
     Who have come from the land of bloody men ;
     Have you borne contempt from any?
     Or what was this which detained you ? "

CHILDREN OF UISNEACHAN.

13. " There was keeping us out from thee,—
     To us, bloody was the rout—
     The king Mac Rosnaich, Chief of the men of Fail,
     Having taken and overcome us."

DEIRDRI.

14   " Where were your heroic weapons,
And your hands—smart and bloody ;
When you allowed—yourselves hale—
To Mac Rosaich to defeat you ? "

CHILDREN OF UISNEACHAN.

15.   " Sleep we did in our ship—
The three brothers, back to back ;
Before we perceived ill or guile,—
The sixteen ships surrounded us."

DEIRDRI.

16.   "Did I not tell you—loved Uisneachan Children,
That hands on the bosoms of women—
And giving way to sleep ;
Did not advance winning in war."

CHILDREN OF UISNEACHAN.

17.   " And though there were no war beneath the sun,
But a man far from his own land ;—
A long sleep—little its delight,
To a man who is in exile.

18.   " Exile—woe to him whose fate it is ;—
Its wont is to have a share of wandering ;—
Little its honour—great its control ;—
Woe to the man whose fate is exile !

19.　" However, there they put us,—
　　　In a dirty cave under the ground ;
　　　Where the salt water would come below us,
　　　Three nine times every day.

20.　" But one good daughter that the king had,—
　　　She had much compassion on us ;
　　　The whole of her father's hides—
　　　Numerous were their hinds and heifers' skins ;
　　　She put between us and the cold water ;—
　　　The fair maiden of best sense ;—
　　　But her father was wont to be in the Red Branch,
　　　And all his friends about him."

THE KING.

21.　" Attend to my whisper, O Tierval,—
　　　The secrecy of women is not good ;—
　　　They will tell in a nook what they hear."

TIERVAL.

22.　" What secret should it be,
　　　That thou wouldst not tell to thy one daughter,—
　　　And the secret that I should get from thee,—
　　　That I would keep, for a year fondly,
　　　Under the border of my right breast ;
　　　And the secrets that I should get from others ;
　　　Dear father, that I would tell to thee."

THE KING.

23. " The king of Erin has sent word, by sea,
To the nobles of Barr-Fail,
That I should receive the full of my ship,
Of gold, and of wares, and of treasure,
For sending the captives, in good faith,
On the Irish Sea, to-morrow."

24. But the maiden heavily sighed,
Very greatly, from her heart ;—
The rafters of the house responded,
To the sighing of the maiden. ·

THE KING.

25. " Who have so heavily sighed ?—
They are sorry for the captives."

TIERVAL.

" 'Twas I that so heavily sighed,—
Thy captives I do dislike.

26. " There is a piercing stitch in my left side,--
And it would kill fifty kings ;—
And there is great beating of my heart,
In the other side opposite the stitch."

H

27. But she came to us with intelligence—
    The Tierval of whitest skin—

CHILDREN OF UISNEACHAN.

" Wert thou over in yon Dun ?—
Or what is said there about us ?"

TIERVAL.

28. " I was over in yon Dun,
    And woful is what is said there of you ;—
    That my father shall obtain the full of his ship,
    Of gold, of wares, and of treasure,
    For putting the captives, without guile,
    On the Irish sea to-morrow.

29. " But your legs stretch towards me,
    So that the locks I can measure ;—
    That I leave not a bit of them neglected,
    In length, in breadth, and in deepness."

30. She went to the smith of the meadow,—
    A smith's hammer was found in his hand,—
    Ever striking it on an anvil.

SMITH.

31. " It is strange to me, king's daughter,
    To travel at night, in time of sleeping ?"

TIERVAL.

"What should make me travel nightly,
Gives thee the right of asking."

SMITH.

32. "It is a blessing that I live,
When I have the right of asking;
When this black head upon my neck,
Was by thee preserved to me.

33. "I was, a day, pounding gold,
In thy father's smithy, in Cluny;
I was accused of the gold that was stolen,—
And such was a story on an enemy."

TIERVAL.

34. "It was the gold ring that I gave thee
That kept thy head over thy shoulders.

35. "To mirth I gave way in my ship,
On a heavy, stormy sea,—
My father's keys fell overboard—
Pity I was not in their stream-pursuit."

36. But he rose up, the smith of Cluny,
The son of the wright from the Red Branch;

And he made the three victorious keys,
In the short time of one half hour.

TIERVAL

37. " Let not a word escape thy lips—
Early or late, or about evening ;
Unless that black hearth speak it,
Or the anvil on which thou madest them."

38. But she came again to inform us—
The Tierval of the curly locks.

TIERVAL.

39. " Stretch towards me your legs,
That I may loosen them ;
In case, I may have forgot the part of them,
In length, in breadth, or in deepness."

40. Then Nais raised his foot on a hacking-stick—
Ard and Ailly equally soon.

TIERVAL.

41. " The three very worthy brothers ;—
Are you now on your feet ?—
Or are there below who can overcome you ?—

CHILDREN OF UISNEACHAN.

42. "If we had our three swords,
And provisions for five nights;
Wax light, half as half,
So as to see each other's faces."

43. She went to seek the three swords,—
To find them was not easier to do;
She went to the servant man of the chamber,—
The fresh maiden, encompassed with amber.

CHAMBER MAN.

44. "'Tis strange, O king's daughter,
To travel, at night, in time of sleeping?"

TIERVAL.

"What makes me travel nightly,
Gives thee the right of asking.

45. "Let me not do the justice of defending—
Daughter of the king from Dun-Meara;—
I seek the three swords,
And five nights' provision
Wax light, half as half;
So that we might see each other's faces."

CHAMBER MAN.

46. "What shouldst thou do with a sword,
Thou highly noble king's daughter?

When thou couldst not, with it, fight a battle,
Or give, with it, a day's service."

TIERVAL.

47.   " I would give a sword of them, as gift,
       To a son that a king had by a fair young woman ;
       I would give another sword of them,
       To the best rider of the mild horses:

48.   " I would give another sword of them,
       To the chief captain of my ship."
       She laid nine pieces of gold
       On the table, for the three swords.

CHILDREN OF UISNEACHAN.

49.   " She, our three swords, brought us,
       And, for five nights, provision ;
       A kind of wax, half as half,
       That we might see each other's faces."

50.   Then, she came to tell us—
       The Tierval of whitest skin :—

TIERVAL.

       " My father has a ship on sea,
       Before him, over, at Cluan Ciaran.

51.   " Five men keeping the ship,—

One tall man above every man,
And he would overcome a hundred in battle.

52.　" But if you encounter him,
Without fear or false dismay ;
Strike properly and well,
Your three swords in one joint."

CHILDREN OF UISNEACHAN.

53.　" Though dark and black the night was,
We did not row roughly ;—
We struck properly and well,
Our three swords in his one joint.

54.　" Come thou in into thy ship,
O Tierval, who art dear to us ;
And not one woman shall go above thee,
But one woman, in the land to which thou goest."

TIERVAL.

55.　" What one woman should it be ?—
When 'tis I who have won you the souls ;—
It would be reckless in me to do that,—
When so many king's sons seek me ;
Were I to depart with hasty steps
For the sake of a foreign company."

CHILDREN OF UISNEACHAN.

56   " They will read of thee, O Clear-white
     If true, that thou art pregnant ;—
     If it be a son or a daughter,
     It will be named to the men of Erin."

TIERVAL.

57.   " I am one daughter to the king,—
     Greater, on that account, is my esteem ;
     But bad is the labourer, who, for a while,
     Should not bring one bird to a haven.

58.   " But I shall stay a year on thy love,
     And another year without tidings of thee ;
     At the end of the fifth or sixth year,
     Come then to seek me from my father,
     And I will keep thy peace for thee,
     From the King of the World and from Conchovar.

PART II.

Lament of Deirdri.

And after informing Deirdri of these matters, she
was much displeased with them, on account of leaving
Tierval behind them, considering that she showed them
so much kindness; that in consequence of her goodness
to them, she should never seek to be above her. Then
Deirdri and they took their departure to seek her; and
Deirdri had a dream.

DEIRDRI.

1. A dream I had last night,
   Of the three sons of the king of Barrachaoil;
   To be fettered and put in the grave,
   By Conchovar from the Red Branch.

CHILDREN OF UISNEACHAN.

2. "But lay thy dream O Deirdri,
   On the steeps of the high eminences,—
   On the mariners of the sea, outside,—
   And on the rough grayish stones;
   But we will get peace, and give it,
   From the King of the World and from Conchovar.

3.   " But as early as the day had come,
       And that the mist was dispelled behind us ;
       Where did our fleet come to land ?—
       But under the door of the high king."

4.   Conchovar himself came out,
       And nineteen hundred men with him ;
       And he asked boldly and hastily,—
       Who are these hosts on the fleet ?

CHILDREN OF UISNEACHAN.

5.   " They are the children of thy own sister,
       And they are sitting on a seat of trouble."

CONCHOVAR.

6.   " You are not sister's children of mine,—
       It is not such a deed you have done me ;—
       But having affronted me, with guile,
       In presence of the men of Erin."

CHILDREN OF UISNEACHAN.

7.   " What ! although we took from thee thy wife,—
       Well-shaped, round-handed, white Deirdri ;
       We did to thee another little kindness,
       And this is the time for its remembrance.

8.   " The day that thy ship burst, at sea,
       Full of gold and of silver ;

We gave thee our own ship,
And we swam ourselves, on sea, around thee."

CONCHOVAR.

9. "Had you done me fifty kind deeds,
Truly, upon my thanks;
Your peace you should not receive in distress,—
But every one great want I could inflict."

CHILDREN OF UISNEACHAN.

10. "We did another little kindness to thee,—
And this were the time for its remembrance;
The day the speckled horse failed thee,
On the green of Dun-Dealgan ;—
Now, we gave thee the gray horse,
Which would bring thee fast to the road."

CONCHOVAR.

11. "Had you done me fifty kind deeds,
Truly, upon my thanks;
Your peace you should not receive in distress,
But every one great want that I could inflict."

CHILDREN OF UISNEACHAN.

12. "We did thee another kind deed,—
And this is the time for its remembrance;—

You owe us numerous obligations,—
Strong is our right to thy succour.

13.   " The time when Murrough Mac Brian,
Fought the seven battles in Binn Eadair;
We brought thee, without failing,
The heads of the sons of the king of the South-east."

CONCHOVAR.

14.   "Had you done me fifty kind deeds,—
Truly, upon my thanks ;
Your peace you should not get in distress,—
But every one great want that I could inflict."

DEIRDRI.

15.   " Arise O Nais, and seize thy sword,—
Good son of the king, of thorough guard ;
Why should his fine body get,
But one turn of the soul."

16.   Nais fixed his heels firmly,
And seized his sword in his fist ;
And fierce was the conflict of the heroes,
Falling on each side of a board.

17.   The Sons of Uisneach fell in the contest,
Like three branches growing so finely,

Destroyed by a dreadful tempest,
Which left neither bud nor spray of them.

CONCHOVAR.

18. "Your death is not, now to me a death,
Children of Uisneachan—unaged ;
Since he fell by you, without guile,
The third noble horseman of Erin.

19. " Move Deirdri out of thy ship,—
Fresh branch of the brown eyelashes;
And thy bright face need not fear,
Hatred, jealousy, or rebuke."

DEIRDRI.

20. " I will not go out of my ship,
Till I obtain my choice of request ;
'Tis no land, or earth, or food ;
It is not three brothers of clearest hue ;
It is not gold, or silver, or horses;—
Neither am I a proud woman ;
But leave to go to the strand,
Where the Children of Uisneach are at rest,
That I might give them the three honey kisses,
To their white, beautiful bodies."

21. They loosed her soft brown-yellow hair,
    Around the maiden so well-formed,
    And her clothes, to the tips of her toes,
    Least she should take away, in stealth,
    As much as the eye of a needle;—
    But one gold ring which was on her finger—
    That she put in her mouth,—
    And she went off with it to the strand,
    Where the Children of Uisneachan were,—
    And she found a wright making oars—
    His knife in the one hand, ·
    And his axe in the other.

DEIRDRI.

22. "O wright, the best I've ever seen,
    For what wouldst thou give the knife?
    What I should give you for it,
    Is the one victorious ring of Erin."

23. The wright desired the ring,
    On account of its fineness and beauty;
    The knife was given to Deirdri,
    And she reached the place of her wish.

24. She then walked to the strand,
    Where were the Children of Uisneach;

And what she found there doubtless,
Their three corpses stretched so long.

DEIRDRI.

25. "No joy without the Children of Uisneach,—
O mournful it is to be without you ;—
Three king's sons who would avenge exiles
Who are speechless at the grave's breast.—

26. "The three bears of the Isle of Britain,—
The three hawks of *Slieve Gullion ;*
The three to whom would yield, heroes,
And whom fierce men would honour.

27. "The three birds of finest hue,
That came over the sea of storms ;   [pillar-stone ;
The three sons of Uisneach from the round
Three ducks swimming on a wave.

28. "I forsook, joyfully, Ulster,
With the three champions that I liked best ;—
My life after them, shall not be long,—
Another man shall not be mine.

29. "The three thongs of those hounds,
Drew a sigh from my heart ;—

'Tis I that should have the treasure,—
Seeing them is cause for sorrow.

30   " O Children of Uisneachan, over yonder—
Lying sole to sole ;
Were the dead to shrink from another living,
You would shrink from me.

31.   " O three brave men from Dun-monny !—
O three youths of victorious virtues !—
After the three, live I will not ;—
Three by whom my haters should be vanquished.

32.   " When their graves you open,
Do not make them uneasy ;—
Let me be close to the grave,
Where no woe or wail is uttered.

33.   " Their three shields and their three lances,
In their narrow bed, place them ;
Their three steel swords, lay them
Stretched above the grave of the tender men.

34.   " Their three hounds and their three falcons,—
Hunters shall be for ever wanting—
Lay near the chiefs of battle,—
The three foster sons of victorious Connel.

35. "Oh, woful is my looking on them,—
    Cause of my distress and sorrow,—
    That I was not put beneath the earth,
    Before the white sons of Uisneach were slain.

36. " I am Deirdri without joy,
    Now bringing to an end, my life ;—
    I give, with my heart, my three kisses,
    And I close, in grief, my days."

37. She then stretched her side to his side,
    And put her lips to his lips,
    And she put the black knife through her heart,
    And she died without regret ;—
    But she threw the black knife in the sea,
    Lest the wright should be blamed.

38. Conchovar reached the strand,
    Along with five hundred, to meet his wife ;
    What he found there, without doubt, was,
    The four bodies stretched down at their length.

CONCHOVAR.

39. " A thousand curses—a thousand woes,—
    On the sense that holds me ;—
    On the sense which made me,
    Slay the fine children of my own sister.

I

40. "They are without life,
       And I am without having Deirdri ;—
       But I will bury in one grave,
       Nais and Deirdri in one bed ;—
       And the little weed that will come through the
       Whoever puts a knot on its top,—   [grave,
       His shall be the choice of a sweetheart.

41. " Were I to be in Newry of victories,
       This night, though cold be the weather ;
       I would put a knot on its top,
       Although the tree were to wither."

Freich Son of Feich.

Auctor Hujus in Keich O Cloan.

1. A friend's sigh from Freich's retreat,—
   A warrior's sigh from *Castle of death;*
   A sigh that would grieve a man,
   And that would make a young woman weep.

2. Here, east, is the cairn under which,
   Is Freich son of Feich of soft hair ;
   He who did kindness to Mave,
   And from whom Cairn Freich is named.

3. Lament of one woman on Cruachan East,—
   About the woman—sad the tale ;—
   'Tis he that heavily, makes her sigh,—
   Freich son of Feich of old strifes.

4. That one woman who wails,
   Going after him to Freich's retreat;—
   Is the maiden of the noble curling locks—
   Daughter of Mave, by heroes sought.

5. Daughter of Orla of golden hair,
   And Freich, to-night, side by side ;
   Although loved by many men,—
   None did she love but Freich.

6.   Mave finds, in her hate,
     The friendship of Freich—man of her sighs ;—
     The cause of his body's wound,—
     Without committing with her, guilt.

7.   She urged him on to his death,
     As women prone to evil do;
     Great was the harm done by Mave,—·
     I tell it, without guile, just now.

8.   There was a rowan tree on Loch May,—
     We see the strand to its south;
     Every quarter—every month,
     There was on it, ripe fruit.

9.   Satisfying was that rowan tree,—
     Sweeter than honey was its bloom ;
     Its red berries would sustain,
     A man without food for nine hours.

10. It would add a year to a man's life—
     That is proved a true tale ;
     It was relief to the diseased,
     The benefit of the fruit when red.

11. After it there was bad luck,—
     Whatever leech would succour men ;

A venomous beast was at its root,
Which, going to pluck it, they had to fight.

12. She was in very ill health,
    The daughter of Athach of free horns ;
    She sent a message for Freich;
    Who inquired of her what was wrong?

13. Mave said she could not be whole,
    Unless she got the full of her soft palm,
    Of the berries of the cold lake,—
    And no one to pluck them, but Freich.

14. Fruit-gathering I never handled,
    Said son of Feich of red cheeks,
    Though sharply it will handle Freich,
    Go I to pluck berries for Mave.

15. Freich moves—the man of fight,
    From us, to swim on the lake ;
    He found the monster sound asleep,
    And its head up to the bush.

16. Freich son of Feich, of weapon sharp,
    Came off from the beast unknown
    Of red berrres, he, a burden, brought,
    Where Mave was, for her relief.

17.   "What thou hast brought with thee—so far good,"—
      Averred Mave of white form;—
      "'T will not relieve me, O strong champion,—
      But to pluck a sprig from the root."

18.   Freich agreed—not a timid youth—
      To swim again on the soft lake;
      And he might not though great his valour,
      Escape death, which was his fate.

19.   He takes the rowan tree by the top,
      Pulls the tree from its root;
      Taking his feet to the land,—
      Again, he was by the beast perceived.

20.   Seizes him while he swims,
      And takes his hand into its wide mouth;
      He takes her by the jaw,—
      Woe 'tis that Freich had not his knife.

21.   The maiden of the noble curling hair,
      Reached him with a golden knife;
      The monster mangled his white skin,
      And his hand was soon lopped off.

22.   They fell, sole to sole,
      On the strand of the round stones, by south

Freich son of Feich and the beast,—
Woe! O God, what that short space did !

23. Fighting her—was not a short fight;—
He took with him her head in his hand;
When he was by the maiden seen,
She fainted upon the strand.

24. The maiden rises from the swoon,—
Takes the hand—'twas a soft hand ;—

MAIDEN.

" Though this is a share for the birds,—
Great was the deed it did below "

25. From that death which the man had got,
Loch May continued the name of the lake ;
That is its name ever since,—
So called down to this time.

26. Then was carried to Freich's retreat,
The corpse of the hero with a *Death's Castle;*
The glen was called by his name,—
Pity ! those who live to tell it.

27. The cairn at hand—this cairn to my side,—
Near to it a hero lived ;—
A man who was not overcome in strength,—
A man whose vigour was fiercest in fight.

28.   Beloved the lips that scorned not friends,—
       To which women kisses gave ;
       Beloved the chief of hosts
       Beloved the cheek redder than rose.

29.   Blacker than the raven, the top of his hair,—
       Redder his cheek than calf's blood ;—
       Softer than the foam of a stream,—
       Whiter than snow, the skin of Freich.

30.   More curled than dewlap his locks,—
       Bluer his eye than ice sheet ;—
       Redder than rowan berries his lips,— ˙
       Whiter his teeth than woodbine bloom.

31.   Higher his spear than a mast,—
       Sweeter than a music-string his voice ;—
       A better swimmer than Freich,
       Streatched not his side to a stream.

32.   Broader than a door was his shield,—
       Beloved the chief to whose back it was ;
       As long as his blade was his arm,—
       Broader was his sword than a ship's board.

33. Pity, it was not in warrior's fight,
That Freich, the giver of gold, fell;
Mournful that—to fall by a beast,—
Pity, O God, he's not still alive.

Conlacb.

Gille-calum Mac an Ollaimh wrote down this tale.

———

Transliterated from Dr. Mac Lauchlan's Transcript of Dean Mac Gregor's Book.

Quatrains 24, 25, 26, 27, 30, and 31, are from Gillies' Collection of Gaelic Songs and Poems.

———

1. I've heard, from very old times,
   A tale which belongs to sorrow;
   To relate it sadly it's time,
   As of us, it is required.

2. The Clanna Rury, of mature judgements,
   Under Conchovar and Connel;
   Gallant were their youths, in the field,
   On the plains of Ulster province.

3. None, joyfully, had come home,
   Of all the warriors of Banva;
   In a battle, fought, another time,
   The Clanna Rury were victorious.

4. There came to us—haughty in his rage—
   The valiant champion, Conlach,
   To reconnoitre our beautiful plains
   From *Dun-Scathaigh* to Erin.

5. Conchovar spoke to the rest—
   " Whom have we got for the youth,
   To obtain knowledge of his news,
   And not to be refused ? "

6. Connel moves, whose hand was not weak,
   To get his tale from the stripling ;
   By the sure pull of the warrior,
   Connel was bound by Conlach !

7. The warrior did not halt with the handling
   Of Connel of furious wrath ;
   A hundred of our host were bound by him —
   A marvel to recount which is lasting.

8. A messenger was sent to the Chief of the *Con*,
   From the wise over-king of Ulster,
   To Dundalgin, sunny and fair—
   The prudent dun of the Gaels.

9. From that dun of which we speak
   Of the prudence of the daughter of Forgall,

Comes the subtle doer of relief,
To the generous king of the lands.

10. The men of green Ulster were asked—
The *Cú* of the Red Branch comes ;—
White-toothed son, his cheeks like red berries,
Refused not to come to our succour.

11. " Long ", said Conchovar to the *Cú* ;
" Wert thou in coming to our succour,
And Connel of brisk chargers,
In bonds, and a hundred of our host ! "

CONNEL.

12. " Hard is it for me to be a captive
O ! man, who would aid a friend ! "

CUCHULLIN.

" Easy it's not to meet his feat sword,—
He who has bound Connel ! "

CONNEL.

13. " Don't think of not going against him
O ! king of detested blue blades !
O ! firm hand, not weak 'gainst anyone,
Think of thy foster-father fettered ! "

14. Cuchullin of the charmed smooth blades,
When he heard the wail of Connel,
Went, with his strength of hands,
To obtain his news from the youth.

CUCHULLIN.

15. "Tell us, come to thy encounter,
O! Prince, wouldst thou shun conflict?
Smooth form of the black eye-lashes,—
Knowledge of the place? Who are thy kindred?"

CONLACH.

16. "Of my spells coming from home,—
Not to tell a tale to a stranger;
Were I to tell it to another,
I would to thy appearance."

CUCHULLIN.

17. "Fight with me thou must needs,
Or, as a friend, must tell thy story;
Take thy choice, O! weak youth;
To encounter me is imprudent."

CONLACH.

18. "But let it not be thought of,
O! valiant Leopard of Erin!

O heroic arm in attack !
That my fame were thine for nothing."

19. They rushed towards each other,—
    The fight is unwomanly ;—
    The stripling received his death-wound—
    The foster-son, hardy and active.

20. Cuchullin and strenuous fight
    Were that day without success ;
    Ah ! his one son was by him slain—
    The noble, brave, fine, green sprig !

CUCHULLIN.

21. " Tell us," said *Cú* of the feats,
    " Since thou art ever, in our power,
    Thy place and thy name precisely ;—
    Do not conceal them from us."

CONLACH.

22. " I am Conlach, son of the *Cú*,
    Lawful heir of Dundalgin ;—
    I am the secret left in the womb,
    Whilst thou wert with Scathach learning.

23. " Seven years was I, in the East,
    Learning war feats from my mother ;

The feats wherewith I've been slain,
Were wanting in my training."

CONLACH.

24. " Take thou with thee my spear,
And pull this shield off me,
And take with thee my steel sword,—
A blade which I received polished,

25. " To my mother bear my curse,
As 'twas she who laid me under spells
And who brought on my suffering ;—
O ! Cuchullin, 'twas by thy doing.

26. "O ! comely white-belted Cuchullin,
Who break'st every knot of danger,
Look, as I have lost my vision,
On which finger the ring is.

27. " Ill wouldst thou understand from me,
Noble, stubborn father ;
How I did throw, weakly aslant,
The spear directly endwise."

28. Cuchullin thought, when died
His son, in the hue of sorrow ;
Reflection, truly was the hero's joy;—
His memory and sense forsook him.

29.   His honour from the body of the *Cú*,
       By his grief was nearly disjoined.
       On seeing at the back of the glen,
       The warrior of Dundalgin.

CUCHULLIN.

30.   " Were I and Conlach living and sound.
       Playing at feats of battle ;
       We should win a strong enviable fight
       Over the men of Alba and Erin.

31.   " A hundred griefs have environed me,
       My being sad, is, no wonder ;
       From my fighting with my one son,
       My wounds to-night are many."

❧ Annotations. ❧

K

ANNOTATIONS

PRECEDING BALLADS.

AN GARBH MAC STAIRN—The Rough, Son of Noise.   Although it is related in traditional story that he was a Norseman, the name is purely Gaelic.

The lines and stanzas which are wanting in Mac-Nicol's variant, assuming it to be the better, are supplied from Fletcher's variant, without, however, making any alteration on the lines or stanzas except such as were required by correct orthography.   None of these variants can be properly divided into quatrains; so the fused ballad is divided into stanzas of such a number of lines as the sense requires.

In O' Reilly's Irish Dictionary the definition of *Cù* is, "s.m. a moth, an insect that gnaws clothes; s.m.

and f. a dog, a gray-hound; s.m. a champion, a hero, a warrior." Here are three words different in meaning and gender—in fact, homonyms. The second word *Cú*, a hound or dog, is cognate with Latin, Greek, Sanskrit, and other Aryan names for the same animal; the third word *Cú*, a champion, a hero, a warrior, is, probably, of pre-Aryan origin, and it borrowed the Aryan declension of *Cú*, a hound. In Gaelic, the names of beasts are given to men, such as *Sionnach*, Fox; *Faolan*, young Wolf, *Onnchú*, Leopard, &c.; but these names are not localised, as in such names as *Cú-Uladh*, Cu of Ulster; *Cú-Connacht*, Cu of Connaught; *Cú-Midhe*, Cu of Meath; *Cú-mara*, Cu of Sea, &c. Among a hundred which Major Condor gives of Hittite or Kheta words, Ku is given as denoting king. " Hittite *Ku*, king; Akkadian *uk* and *ku*, king; Susian *Ku*, king; Manchu *chu*, lord." (*"On the early races of Western Asia," by Major C. R. Condor, R. E. Journal of the Anthropological Institute, August, 1889.*)

In this ballad Cuchullin calls himself king in reply to Garbh.

GARBH.

" I give a king's oath on it,
Handsome men of Erin,
That I will not go into my ship
Without homage from Cuchullin."

CUCHULLIN.

"I give another king's oath,"
It is what the high armed Cú spoke
"That thou shalt not take my homage on sea,
While I am myself in life."

Here, be it observed, Cuchullin, as *Cú* calls himself king.

CU-CHULAINN. Traditional Irish History informs us that Cuchullin had several names. First he was named Setanta, and the cause of his getting the name of Cuchullin is the source of a strange legend, related in several very old Irish books, among which is *Lebor na h-Uidhre*, The Book of the Dun Cow; so named because bound in the skin of a dun cow. At one time Culand, an extraordinary artificer in metals, who resided and had his forge near Slieve Gullion in Armagh, came to the palace of Emania to bid king Conor MacNessa and the Red Branch Knights to a feast. Setanta, then a small boy was bidden, as it occurred that he was on a visit at the palace at this very time; howbeit, when the company set off he continued behind to finish a game of ball with his companions, and said he would follow quickly. He went off in the evening, and came late to Culand's house; but when he tried to enter the house, he found the way obstructed by a huge dog which the artificer kept to protect his premises at night. The fierce beast instantaneously attacked him; but the valiant little fellow, without feeling the slightest terror, gallantly defended himself. When the terrific uproar outside, was heard by Culand and his guests ; the smith, in great alarm, started up and inquired whether any of the company had stayed behind ; for he said, none had ever come near the house at night without being torn to pieces by the dog. Then the king instantly remembered how Setanta had promised to follow him, and Fergus Mac Roigh and several other of the guests, hurried out to save him, notwithstanding, when they came to the place, they found the large dog lying dead, and the juvenile champion standing over him. Fergus, highly delighted snatched up the boy triumphantly on his shoulders, carried him into the house, and placed him on the floor in presence of the king and all the assembly, who received him with enthusiastic joy.

Culand, subsequently to his having at first given vent to his gratification at the boy's escape, forthwith fell to grieving for his dog, without which he complained that his house and flocks would now be unprotected. Young Setanta, however, said that he would provide him with a puppy of the same breed, were it possible to find one in all Erin, from *Tonn Tuath* in the north to the Wave of Cleena in the south ; and he offered, besides, to take charge of protecting the house at night until the young dog should be grown enough to supply his place. . Then the king's druid, Cathbad, who was present, proposed that the boy's name should be altered to *Cu-Chulaind* (Culand's hound) ; and he predicted that he should be known by this name to all generations to come, and that his fame and celebrity would live to the end of the world among the men of Erin and Alba. In this story it is said that Culand's house and forge were near Slieve Gullion in Armagh, which is in Irish *Sliabh g-Cuillinn* Mountain, the same name is in Albanic Gaelic *Sliabh Cuilinn*. O' Reilly's Irish Dictionary gives *cuileann* which is the same as the Albanic name. The two l-sounds, l as in *Culand* and l as in *Cuileann* are, sometimes, met with in two forms of the same word. In O' Reilly's Irish Dictionary we have *Fulangaim*, I suffer and *Fuileamhuin,* suffering ; the l sounding in the former as in *Culand*, and in the latter as in *Cuileann*. In MacLeod and Dewar's Gaelic Dictionary occur *Fuiling*, suffer, bear, endure, and *Fulaing*, suffer, bear, endure. These two words, identical in meaning, were, no doubt, originally, one of these two forms, or a form from which they have been derived, and which is now obsolete. The same may be said of the fabulous name Culand and of the Gaelic names for holly, *cuileann* and *cuillion*. So it is very likely that *Cu-chulainn* is identical with *Cu-chuilinn*, that is Cú of the holly or holly-wood of Slieve Gullion.

MacNicol's variant begins with :—

> *Erich a Chu 'n Teridh.*
> Arise O Cu of Tara.

Fletcher's begins with :—

> *Eirich a Righ na Teimhre.*
> Arise O King of Tara.

Teridh and Teimhre are two genitives differing from the correct genitive *Teamhrach* whereof the nominative is Teamhair, which signifies, as an adjective, pleasant, and as a substantive, a covered or shaded walk on a hill for a convenient prospect. Dr. Joyce tells us that the pronunciation of *teamhrach* is *taragh* or towragh ; but I have heard old rehearsers of old Gaelic poems in Islay and in the Long Island pronounce it *tevrách*, the v nasal, which would seem to be nearest the ancient pronunciation. The Tara of this ballad is Tara in Meath, the seat of the ancient over kings of Ireland. There is a place named Tara in the parish of Witter, Down. It has a fine fort commanding a wide view. There is another in the parish of Durrow, King's County ; and a conspicuous hill near Gorey in Wexford, l-aving a cairn on its top, is called Tara. *Teamhair-Luachra* was a fam us royal seat in Munster; so named from the district of *Sliabh Luachra* (Rushy mountain), or Slieve-leugher. Its exct situation is not known now.

Several parts of both variants of this ballad are very confused and incoherent. *An Garbh* demands entrance to Tara and seeks submission from Cuchullin which is refused, and the consequence is a fight in which *An Garbh Mac Stairn,* (The Rough, Son of Noise), was slain.

"*An Maoidh Gallan nan Corag,*" is the last line in stanza 8 of MacNicol's variant, and the corresponding line in Fletcher's is the last line of stanza 14. "*A' maogh, Gamaim nan goirean.*" *Magh Gallan* may mean the plain of branches, or the plain of youths; and *Magh Gallan nan comhrag* may signify in Albanic Gaelic, plain of the youths of the combats; in Irish *Magh gallán* may denote plain of branches or of pillar-stones. *Gallán,* a pillar-stone, gives name to many places in Ireland, such as Gallan near Ardstraw in Tyrone; Gallans and Gallanes in Cork. In Ulster, there are some low hills, which, on account of a pillar-stone standing on the top, were designated Drumgallan (hill-ridge of pillar-stones), and some of these have given names to townlands. The name of a townland in Tyrone and of a parish in Antrim is Aghagallon, field of the pillar-stone.

Magh Gámain nan Goirean, 'Plain of the long step of the caves.' *Gáman,* a long step. *Goire,* a cave.

"*Mac mhic Cairbre o'n Chraoibh Ruaidh.*"

Son of son of Cairbre from the Red Branch.

A' Chraobh Ruadh, The Red Branch.

Craobh s. f. a tree or branch in modern Irish and in Albanic Gaelic, a tree. In old Irish it is *craebh,* a branch.

Craebh-ruadh, Red Branch was the name of one of the houses in the palace of Emania. The Red Branch Knights of Ulster, (*Curaidhean na Craoibhe Ruaidhe,* literally the Champions of the Red Branch), so extolled in early Irish romances and poems, and whose renown has come down to the present day, flourished in the first century and achieved their greatest glory in the reign of Conchover Mac Nessa. In the said house they were trained to heroism and feats of arms. The name of this military college is commemorated in Creeveroe, the name of the adjacent townland,

The foundation of the renowned palace of *Eamhuin* took place about 300 years before the christian era, and forms an important epoch. The annalist Tighernach assigns it as the limit to authentic Irish history, and

asserts that all accounts of events previous to this, are
unreliable. Here follow the circumstances of its origin as
recorded in the Book of Leinster. Three Kings Aedh-
ruadh (*Ayrooe*, Red-haired Aedh), Dihorba, Ciombaeth
agreed to reign each for seven years in alternate
succession, and they each enjoyed the sovereignty for
three periods, or twenty one years, when Aedh-ruadh
died. The famous Macha of the golden hair, his
daughter, claimed the right of reigning when her
father's turn came. She was opposed by Dihorba
and his sons, but she defeated them in several battles.
In one of them Dihorba was slain, and she then took
to herself the royal sway.

She married, subsequently, the surviving king
Kimbay, and made prisoners of the five sons of
Dihorba. It was proposed by the Ultonians that
they should be put to death:—"Not so," said she,
"because it would be the defilement of the righteous-
ness of a sovereign in me; but they shall be condemned
to slavery, and shall raise a rath around me, and it
shall be the chief city of Ulster for ever." An
imaginary derivation of the name of the palace is given
in the account. "And she marked for them the dun
with her brooch of gold from her neck," so that the
palace was named *Eomuin* or *Eamhuin*, from *eo*, a
brooch and *muin*, the neck. The same explanation of

the name is given in Cormac's Glossary. *(Stoke's
" Three Irish Glossaries," p. 17.)*

The ruins of this spacious palace are situated about
a mile and a half west of Armagh, and consist of a
circular rath or rampart of earth with a deep fosse
which enclose about eleven acres. There are two
smaller circular forts within. The name is probably
derived from the number of these smaller forts, which
is two, equivalent to a couple or a pair; for *Eamhain*
" is an old Gaelic word which signifies two or double;
Da ni eamhnadh, *i.e.* Dubladh, *Double."* "Eamh-
anta, Idem." (Llwyd's Irish-English Dictionary.) Eamhuin, the name of the palace, and *Eamhain*, two or
double, do no differ but extremely little in pronunciation.
The large rath is yet known by the name of the Navan
Fort. The correct Gaelic form is *Eamhuin*, and is
pronounced *aven;* for Emania is merely a Latinised
form. The Gaelic article *an* contracted as it frequently
is to *'n* makes it *'n Eamhuin* which Navan exactly
represents in pronunciation.

In the year 332 this ancient palace was destroyed.
It flourished as the principal royal residence of Ulster
for upwards of 600 years; and it would perhaps not be
an easy matter to identify its site with complete
certainty, were it not for the remarkable tenacity with
which it has kept its name through all the wars,

changes, and social revolutions of sixteen hundred years.

Macha of the golden hair is commemorated by the place-name, *Ardmacha*, height of Macha, anglicised Armagh.

The city of Ardmagh is mentioned in a great number of Irish documents. Some of these are very ancient, such as the Book of Leinster, &c., and at all times, in the form of Ard-Macha, except when this name is Latinised. The most ancient of these is the Book of Armagh. It is known that this book was transcribed about the year 807, and in it the name is translated *Altitudo Machae*, that is Macha's height. The place is spoken of in connection with St. Patrick in this same Book of Armagh, and in several other old authorities. It is recorded that St. Patrick founded the cathedral about the year 457, the site of which was granted to him by Daire, who was the chief of the environing district. The history of St. Patrick and of this foundation is fully accepted as authentic, there is, therefore, reliable evidence for the existence of the name in the fifth century, albeit no document of that age in which it is written is known to exist ; and even without further evidence, it follows, as a consequence, that it is older, as it was in use before St. Patrick's arrival; so St. Patrick accepted the name as he found it.   It is on record that Macha of the golden hair was buried at Armagh.   It was she that founded Emania, and for her, with hardly any doubt, the place was named *Ard-Macha.*   It may, consequently, be inferred as obviously certain that the name is more than 2000 years old.

As has been already remarked, the name, *An Garbh Mac Stairn,* is purely Gaelic, and there is no reference to *Lochlann* or any Scandinavian territories or Scandinavian names, mentioned in old Gaelic tales and poems, in the two variants of this ballad.   It is said of the hero, in Fletcher's variant, that he came from the East to the door of Tara.   It is said in the text of MacNicol's variant that he came from the *Esraidh,* and in a prose paragraph at the end that he came from the *Esra.* In Fletcher's variant it is averred that he came from '*n Ghrèig uamharaidh ro ghairg,* (the very rough horrible Greece), and in another stanza it is recounted that he came from the *Eassa-Roimh,* which would seem to denote the *Waterfalls of Rome*   The main part of the story of the ballad would seem to be much older than the period of the Norse invasions of Ireland and Scotland, and it is probably entirely mythical.

NA CINN—The Heads.   The variant in Dean Mac Gregor of Lismore's Book.   Other variants of this ballad have been collected at different times in different parts of the Highlands. It was in the Ardchonaill MS. collected in 1690. It is in Kennedy's Second Collection, a MS. in the Advocates' Library; it is in Hugh and John MacCallum's Collection of Gaelic Poems and Songs, a book published in 1816. I heard it myself narrated by one Donald MacIntyre in Benbecula, but I do not just now recollect whether it was in the summer of 1859 or of 1860.

This ballad is ascribed by Dean Mac Gregor to *Conall Cearnach Mac Eadarscoil,* Connell the Victorious son of Eiderscheal. Connell was the foster father of Cuchullin. He was one of the knights of the Red Branch, *(Curaidhean na Craoibhe Ruaidhe),* and when Cuchullin was slain, he took revenge upon his enemies by putting all of them to death. Eiderscheal is a very ancient Gaelic personal name. It was the name of the king of Ireland according to Irish Legendary History in the year A.C. 5. and his son Conaire ascended the throne in A.D. 1, who reigned 70 years. The Clan O' h-Edersceoil, anglicised O' Driscoll, are said to be descendants from Aeneas son of Lughach Maccon, the 113th king of Ireland. Edersceal was the name of the Grandson of this Aeneas. The O' Falveys and O' Driscolls were hereditary admirals of Desmond. (Desmond in Gaelic, *Deas-mhumhan,* that is South Munster.

In this ballad Cuchullin is said to be the foster son of *Conall Cearnach* (Connel the Victorious) and the latter his foster father; but in "The Wooing of Emer," whereof a translation by Kuno Meyer is found in Numbers 1, 2, 3, 4 of "The Archæological Review," *Conall Cearnach* (Connell the Victorious) is said to be the foster brother of Cuchullin.   Of this tale the translator, Kuno Meyer tells us, that it "belongs to the oldest, or heroic, cycle of early Irish literature.   Its central figures were the Ulster King Conchobor and Cuchulaind, the hero of this war band, and of the people. Several versions have come down to us, on which see Jubainville, *Catalogue de la Littérature Épique de l' Irlande, p. 227.*   My translation is based on the fragment in the *Lebor na h-Uidhre*, (compiled about 1050 A.D.), and on a complete version in the Stowe MS. 992, (compiled in 1300)." (The Archæological Review, March 1888, p. 68.)

Eimhir, the old form of which is Emer, the wife of Cuchullin, was the daughter of Forgall the Wily. Forgall was much opposed to her being married to Cuchullin; so he used all his wiles to prevail on Cuchullin to undertake such adventures as would lead him to ruin.   Cuchullin was finally successful, after severe trials and much wandering from one region to another, to secure Eimhir for his wife; but before this was accomplished, he killed her brothers, her father, and her paternal aunt. Forgall was a maternal nephew of *Teathra*, the king of the Fomorians.

Th's ballad I have directly transliterated from Dean Mac Gregor's orthography. *Rosk mir erre* is trans- literated by Dr. Mac Lauchlan, "*Rosg mar fheur*," but *erre* is correctly transliterated *eidhre*, ice ; *wrow* trans- literated *bhru* makes no sense, it is clearly an error for chrow—*chruth*, form. The Dean's orthography seems to point to a variety of Highland sub-dialects of Gaelic and to show that he collected the Gaelic poems in his collection in various districts in the Highlands, or from persons who belonged to various districts.

CUCHULAINN 'NA CHARBAD.—Cuchullin in his Chariot. The variant of this ballad taken is that in MacCallum's Collection made in 1813. Cuchullin's gen- ealogy is given as Cuchullainn son of Seimh-suailti son Aodh, son of Agh, son of other Aodh. In "The Wooing of Emer," it is said, "The chariot-chiefs of Ulster were performing on ropes stretched across from door to door in the house at Emain. Fifteen feet and nine score was the size of that house. The chariot-chiefs were performing three feats, viz :—the spear-feat, and the apple-feat, and the sword edge-feat. These are the chariot-chiefs who performed those feats—Connall the Victorious son of Amorgen ; Fergus, son of Roich the Overbold; Loegaire the Victorious, son of Connad; Celtchar, son of Uthider; Dubhthach, son of Lugaid ; Cuchulaind, son of Sualdam ; Scel, son of Barnene, (from whom the pass of Barnene is named), the warder of Emain Macha. From him is the saying "A story of Scel's," for he was a mighty story teller. Cuchulaind surpassed all of them at those feats for quickness, and deftness. The women of Ulster loved Cuchulaind greatly for his quickness at the feats, for the nimbleness of his leap, for the excellency of his wisdom, for the sweetness of his speech, for the loveliness of his look." (The Archæological Review, March 1888, pp. 69, 70.) The name in this variant of the ballad—the second part of it—*suailte* seems to be allied to *Sualdam* the name given to Cuchullin's father in "The Wooing of Emer," as given above. *Suailte* is very likely a corruption of *Sualdam.*

DUAN DHEIRDRI.—Lay of Deirdri. The first part is from Fletcher's Collection made in 1755, and published in J. F. Campbell's *Leabhar na Fèinne,* and from Dr. Irvine's MS. collected in 1801. Both MSS. are deposited in the Advocates' Library, and the variants for J. F. Campbell were copied for him by Malcolm Macphail. Here what is wanting in Fletcher's variant is supplied from Dr. Irvine's. The second part is partly from Fletcher's and from Dr.

Irvine's. Her grief over the bodies of the heroes is from Stewart's *Aoidheadh Chlainn Uisnich*, being the concluding stanzas in Stewart's variant. After giving utterance to these sad words she assassinated herself, and threw the knife she got from the carpenter into the sea least he should be found fault with. The last portion altogether is Conchovar's lament for his nephews the sons of Uisneachan, a name always found in the genitive form. The forms of which vary—these are Usnech, Usnach, Usnachan, Usnech, Usnech, in the wooing of Emer. In some Island in Alba, (Scotland now), Scathach a warrior woman had her dùn, where she taught feats of war to young heroes. Some versions relate that a crowd of the warriors of Erinn were in that dùn learning feats from Scathach, and among them Noise son of Usnech. "But it is not told in this version that they were there at that time." ("The Wooing of Emer," Archæological Review, June 1888, p. 299.)

In the beginning of Fletcher's variant it is said that the sons of Uisneachan went to Dubh-Lochlann, and left Deirdri in Alba with a youth to attend her named *An Gille dubh*, The Black Lad. O'Reilly defines *Dubhlochlanach* a Dane. Scandinavia is translated at the end of Spurrell's English-Welsh Dictionary *Dulychlyn* In Gaelic *Lochlann* is the name for Norway and Denmark, and extended at one time to Northern Germany. *Loch* signifies black or dark, and probably *Lochlann* signifies black or dark land; land in which there is but little sunlight.

"It is well-known that Scadinavia (agreeing with the O.E. Icedining), is the true form of the name which appears in the current text of Pliny as Scandinavia. The etymology of this name or rather of the first element, has been sought by Mullenhoff in Lappish, but the evidence on which he relied was regarded by Dr. Wilhelm Thomson as insecure. I would suggest that the name may be explained plausibly from Germanic sources. Skadino is the exact phonological equivalent of *skoreinoz*, (c. f. shade); so that skadina a (h) w ja may possibly have meant "the dark Island." The alternative form Skadnya—apparently implied in the Scandia, Scandza of Ptolemy and Jordanes, and in the O.N. Skani—may be a parallel derivative from the same root. There seems to be some reason for thinking that Skadinavia was originally the name of an imaginary island in the extreme north, the mythical primitive seat of the Germanic race. The notion that the regions of the far north were wrapt in perpetual darkness prevailed widely in antiquity and is easily accounted for. Reports of the long nights of northern lands would naturally give rise to the inference that in

countries more remote from the sun, the night would be perpetual. The hypothesis of an original mythical reference in the name is not however absolutely necessary to justify the derivation which I have proposed, the Scandinavia of historical geography might very naturally have been called "the isle of darkness" by those who dwelt further south."—(*The Academy*, June 28, 1870. HENRY BRADLEY.)

Sorch, clear, bright. *Sorcha*, light. Sorchir-Sorcha-thir, land of light, the southwest of Europe, and the south in general, contrasts with Lochlann.

Righ Bharrachoil. The father of Clann Usnech is so designated in Fletcher's variant of the ballad *Barr a' chaoil*, the top of the sound or strait, or perhaps his kingdom was a narrow strip of land. The name suits either explanation. Naois is *noise* in 'The Wooing of Emer,' and *Naisi* in older writings. At p. 33 of the *Journal of the Anthr. Institute, August 1889*, Major Conder in his paper on the "Early Races of Western Asia," says 'Nazi is a Susian and Akkadian word which is spelt syllabically, and signifies a prince.' This word closely resembles the Old Gaelic *Naisi* who according to the story of the Sons of Usnach was a prince, and there is reason to believe that numerous Gaelic words and names are of pre-Keltic origin and Turanian. Major Conder tells us—" My comparisons have been carried from China to Etruria, and from Finland to Chaldea; from the earliest days, 3000 B.C. down to the present day; and the net result is that the Turko-Tartar languages serve best to explain both the geographical and the personal names of the Hittites."

The name *Ainle* has been changed in more modern variants to Aille, and Naisi has become Snaois and Snais in some cases. Deirdri is sometimes Deirdir and Deardra. *A' Chraobh Ruadh*, The Red Branch is frequently mentioned. The smith who supplied the knife to Deirdri is said to have been son to the carpenter of the Red Branch.

Dundealgan. The great fortress now called the moat of Castletown is the Dundealgan of ancient Irish Legendary history and of folklore; the residence of Cuchullin chief of the knights of the Red Branch in the first century. It is called *Dun-Delca* in some of the tales of the *Leabhar na h-Uidhre*, (Book of the Dun Cow); but in less ancient authorities *Dun-Dealgan*, that is to say Dealga's fort; and according to O'Cuiry it received its name from Delga, a Firbolg who built it. The same personal name occurs in Kildalkey in Meath. In one of the Irish charters in the Book of Kells is written *Cill Delga*, Delga's church. This great fortress is a mile inland from the modern Dundalk.

"*Latha catha beinn Eudainn.*" The day of the

battle of the peak of *Eudainn.* *Beinn Eadainn* is the form which *Ben Eadair* takes in Highland versions of tales and poems common for many centuries or perhaps to upwards of a thousand years both to Ireland and Scotland. This small Island appears as Edri Deserta on Ptolemy's map, and as Edrou Herémos in his Greek text *i.e.* the desert of Edros. After the Greek inflection is removed and allowing for the wonted contraction, the original form *Edar* is restored. This is exactly the Gaelic name of Howth used in all ancients Irish authorities, either as it stands, or with the addition of Ben, (*Ben-Edair*, the peak of Edar) ; yet well-known throughout the whole of Ireland by speakers of Gaelic. In accordance with some Irish authorities the place obtained the name of Ben-Edair from a Tuatha De Danann chieftain, Edar, the son of Edgaeth, who was buried there; it is affirmed by others that it was from Edar the wife of Gann, one of the five Firbolg brothers who divided Ireland between them. Howth is a Danish name. It is written in old letters Hofda, Houete, and Howeth. These are all varied forms of the Norse word *hóved*, a head.

The Irish names originally collected for the ancient Phoenician atlas used by Ptolemy, were learned from natives of Ireland by sailors speaking a totally different language. These latter delivered them from memory to the compiler, who had to represent them by Phoenician letters, and they were afterwards transferred by Ptolemy into the Greek language. In such manner were all other ancient names of places in the British Isles collected as well as in other parts of the World by Phoenicians and copied by Ptolemy into his work on Geography, from an old Phoenician atlas.

The country where the sons of Usnach were captured does not seem to have been Scandinavia; for in one variant of the ballad, he is called Niall Mac Frasgain, chief of the men of *fail*. *Fal* signifies a king and *fail* is the genitive. Inis-fáil means Island of king, or King's island, one of the old names of Ireland. *Mac Rosaich* is also called chief of the men of *fail*, which might signify men of the king. "*Uaislean Bharr-Phail*" are spoken of, and here Bharr-Phail may stand for *Bharr-Fáil*, for Upland of King or King's Upland. The father of Tiervail is said to have been often at the Red Branch, and would seem to have been a king in Alban not far from Ireland, for the Irish sea *(Cuan na h-Eireann)* is mentioned, across which the king of Ireland promised to send to Tierval's father a ship load of gold, silver, and valuable goods for the captives whom he wished to obtain. Tiervail rendered her father's plans futile, and enabled the captives to escape. Many things are referred to in the different variants of the ballad.

Beinn Aird or *Beinn Ardre ;* the first named means peak of height and second peak of high plain.

"Righ an Domhain" and Conchobhar are mentioned together. Tiervail is addressed in one variant the daughter of the king from Dun Meara. Murcha Mac Brian is mentioned in connection with the seven battles of Beinn Eadair, as is also Murcha Mac Lir. These are two different persons and seem to belong to other tales.

" Cinn mhic righ na h-Earra-dheise," Heads of the sons of the king of the South-west. The Southwest here may mean the South-west of Ireland, or the South-west of Europe, Spain or Portugal, &c. The name Ailne has been changed in many variants of the ballad to Ailde, Aillbheach, and *Aille,* while Naisi has been changed to Noise, Naois, and Snaois, &c.

"Cinn seachd mic Righ Mòrfhairge," Heads of the seven sons of King of Great Sea. Here, probably, the Mediterranean is meant, and has likely reference to the Fonorians. *Dun-monaidh* was at one time the capital town of the Dalriadic Scots. It is situated in Knapdale, and the ruins have called forth the attention of distinguished antiquarians.

A great many of the variants of Deirdri's Lament have been translated into English. One of these is by Dr. Whitley Stokes, Leipzic, 1887.

(IN) main tír an tír út thoir
Alba con (a) hingantaibh ;
nocha ticfuinn eisdi ille,
omana tisainn le Noise.

IN main Dun fidhgha is Dún-finn
inmain in dun osa cinn,
inmain Inis Draigen de,
is inmain Dun Suibnei.

Caill Cuan,
gair tiged Ainnle, mo núar !
fa gair lim dobi (in) tan,
is Naise an oirear Alban.

Glend Laid !
docollainn fan mboirinn caoimh ;
iasg is sieng is saill bruic
fa hi mo chuid an Glend Laigh.

Glenn Masain!
ard a crimh geal a gasáin ;
donimais collud corrach
os inbir mungaich Masáin.

Glenn Eitci !
ann dotogbhus mo cettig ;

alaind a fidh iar néirghe,
cuaile gréne Glenn Eitchi.

Glenn Urchán!
bahi inglenn diriug dromcháin;
nochor uallcha fer a aoisi,
na Noise an Glenn Urcháin.

Glenn Da Ruadh,
mochen gach fer dána dúal;
is binn guth cúach ar cráib cruim,
ar in mbinn ós Glinn Da Rúadh.

IN main Draigen is trén traigh,
inmain a uisce ingainimh glain;
nocha ticfuinn eisde anoir,
mana tísuinn lem inmain.

Translation of the preceding.

A loveable land (is) yon land in the east,
Alba with its marvels;
I would not come hither out of it,
Had I not come with Naisi.

Loveable are Dún-fidge and Dún-finn,
Loveable the fortress over them;
Loveable Inis Draigende,
And loveable Dún Suibni.

Caill Cuan!
Unto which Ainnle would wend, at last;
It was short I thought the time,
And Naisi in the region of Alba.

Glenn Laid!
I need to sleep under a fair rock;
Fish and venison and badger's fat,
This was my portion in Glenn Laid.

Glenn Masáin!
Tall its garlic, white its branches;
We used to have an unsteady sleep,
Over the grassy estuary of Masán.

Glenn Etive!
There I raised my first house,
Delightful its wood after rising,   .
A cattlefold of the sun is Glenn Etive.

Glenn Urcháin!
It was the straight, fair-ridged glen,

Not prouder was (any) man of his age,
Than Naisi in Glenn Urchain.

Glenn Dá-Rúad!
My love to every man who hath it as an heritage!
Sweet is cuckoo's voice on bending branch,
On the peak over Glenn dá Rúad.

Beloved is Draigen over a strong beach;
Dear its waters in pure sand;
I would not have come from it, from the east,
Had I not come with my beloved.

The best explanation given of the place-names in Deirdri's Valedictory address to Scotland (Alba), of which so many variants exist, is so far as I know, that from p. 337, to p. 345 of Brown's "Memorials of Argyle-shire." Mr. Brown is a native of Cowal himself, and is intimately acquainted with the topography of the district, and he seems to me to show clearly that the place-names mentioned in Deirdri's Valedictory Address to Alba, are Cowal place-names.

Windisch the eminent German-Irish scholar tells us that there are twenty three variants and copies of the tale of Deirdri in Ireland. The Book of Leinster, which was compiled about 1150 contains the earliest complete variant of the tale.

Mr. Brown gives a transcript of the valedictory poems of Deirdri from the Glen Masan Manuscript, at p. 307, as he thinks it is the first variant given of this poem, and follows it by the other variants copied from it.

Dean Mac Gregor heads his variant of this ballad, "Auctor hujus in Keich O Cloan," which transliterated is, Author of this An Caoch O' Cluain. According to what the editor of the Dean's Book says in a foot note to the English translation of this ballad, "Some of the readers of the MS. have made it out to be the name of a woman." This could not be; for no woman's surname can begin with O, anymore than with Mac in Gaelic. It must always be Ni or Nic contractions for daughter; O' means grandson, and Mac, son.

LAOIDH FHRAOICH or *BAS FHRAOICH.* This ballad was at one time very popular everywhere throughout the Highlands. It is found in Mac Nicol's Collection made about 1755; in Gillies, published at Perth in 1786; and in Campbell's West Highland Tales, vol. 3. It is found also in some other collections. I have confined myself in this collection of old Gaelic ballads to the variant of *Fraoch* in the Dean of Lismore's Book. *Caiseal-chro,* denotes Castle of blood literally, the editor of the Dean's Book thinks that it signifies a stone coffin. It may have meant a litter for carrying a mortally wounded hero to a burial place. *Bho* is not often used in old compositions, *o* being more frequent. *Bho* has now, in the greater number of districts almost supplanted *o*, unfavourably often to euphony. *Fithich* the genitive of *Fitheach*, Raven, which seems to have been in old times a man's name; so was also its diminutive *Fitheachan*, for we have a surname *Mac Fhitheachan*, which denotes Son of Little Raven.

"*Do chongfadh a caoran dearg,*
Fear gun bhiadh gu ceann IX traa."

Naoi trátha, Nine hours, not nine meals.

Froth in the Dean's variant is a mistake for frith, which signifies, "profit, gain or advantage"—O' Reilly. *Foirinn* contraction of *foirighthin,* relief, succour—O' Reilly.

The berries of this rowan tree would add a year to a man's life; but a venomous monster was at the root of it, that attacked any person who ventured to pluck the berries; in the Pursuit of "*Diarmuid and Grainne,*" part II., page 11. "What berries are those that Fionn required" asked Grainne, that they cannot be got for him. "They are these," said Diarmuid; the Tuatha De Danaan left a quicken tree in the cantred Ui Fhiachrach, and in all berries that grow upon that tree there are many virtues, there is in every berry of them, the exhilaration of wine, and the satisfying of old mead; and whoever should eat three berries of them, had he completed a hundred years, he would return to the age of thirty years. Nevertheless, there is a giant, hideous and foul to behold, keeping that quicken tree, [he is wont to be] every day at the foot of it, and to sleep every night at the top. Moreover he has made a desert of that cantred round about him, and he cannot be slain until three terrible strokes be struck upon him of an iron club that he has, and that club is thus; it has a thick ring of iron through its end, and the ring around his, [*i.e.* the giant's] body; he moreover has taken as a covenant from Fionn and from the Fenians of Erin not to hunt that cantred, and when Fionn outlawed me and became my enemy, I got of him leave to hunt, but that I should never meddle with the berries. "And O Children of Moirne," quoth Diarmuid, "choose ye between combat with me for my head, and going to seek the berries from the giant." "I swear by the rank of my tribe among the Fenians," said [each of] the children of Moirne, "that I will do battle with thee first."

Thereupon these good warriors, that is the children of Moirne and Diarmuid, harnessed their comely bodies in their array of weapons of valour and battle, and the combat that they resolved on was to fight by the strength of their hands.

Howbeit Diarmuid bound them both upon the spot.

" Thou hast fought that strife well," said Grainne, "and I vow that [even] if the children of Moirne, go not to seek those berries, I will never lie in thy bed unless I get a portion of them, although that is no fit thing for a woman to do; and I shall not live if I taste not those berries."

" Force me not to break peace with the Searbhan Lochlannach," said Diarmuid, " for he would none the more readily let me take them." " Loose these bonds from us," said the children of Moirne, "and we will go with thee, and we will give ourselves for thy sake."

" Ye shall not come with me," said Diarmuid, " for were ye to see one glimpse of the giant, ye would more likely die than live after it." "Then do us the grace," said they "to slacken the bonds on us, and to let us go with thee privately that we may see thy battle with the giant before thou hew our heads from our bodies;" and Diarmuid did so.

Then Diarmuid went his ways to the Searbhan Lochlannach, and the giant chanced to be asleep before him. He dealt him a stroke of his foot, so that the giant raised his head and gazed up at Diarmuid, and what he said was, "Is it that wouldst fain break peace, O son of O' Duibhne?" "It is not that," said Diarmuid, " but that Grainne the daughter of Cormac has conceived a desire for those berries

M

which thou hast, and it is to ask the full of a fist of those berries from thee that I am now come." "I swear," quoth the giant, "were it even, that thou shouldst have no children, but the birth now in her womb, and were there but Grainne of the race of Cormac the son of Art, and were I sure that she should perish in bearing that child, that she should never taste one berry of those berries." " I may not do thee treachery," said Diarmuid, " therefore, I now tell thee, it is to seek them by fair means or foul that I am come upon this visit."

The giant having heard that, rose up and stood, and put his club over his shoulder, and dealt Diarmuid three mighty strokes, so that he wrought him some little hurt in spite of the shelter of his shield. And when Diarmuid marked the giant off his guard he cast his weapons upon the ground, and made an eager, exceeding strong spring upon the giant, so that he was able with his two hands to grasp the club. Then he hove the giant from the earth and hurled him round him, and he stretched the iron ring that was about the giant's head and through the end of the club; and when the club reached him [Diarmuid] he struck three mighty strokes upon the giant, so that he dashed his brains out through the openings of his head and of his ears, and left him dead without life; and two of the Clanna Moirne were looking at Diarmuid as he fought that strife.

When they saw the giant fall they too came forth, and Diarmuid sat him down weary and spent after that combat, and bade the children of Moirne bury the giant under the brushwood of the forest, so that Grainne might not see him, "and after that go ye to seek her, also, and bring her with you." The children of Moirne drew the giant forth into the wood, and put him underground and went for Grainne, and brought her to Diarmuid. "There, O! Grainne," said Diarmuid, "are the berries thou didst ask for, and do thou thyself pluck of them whatever pleases thee. "I swear," said Grainne, "that I will not pluck a single berry of them, but the berry that thy hand shall pluck, O, Diarmuid!" Thereupon, Diarmuid rose and stood, and plucked the berries for Grainne and for the children of Moirne, so that they ate their fill of them.

In this story, the place of the venomous beast is supplied by the giant Searbhan Lochlannach; the rowan berries correspond to the golden apples of the garden of the Hesperides, to take which, was one of the labours of Hercules. Fraoch killed the venomous animal, and was killed himself in the strife. Diarmuid killed the giant Searbhan Lochlannach, and procured the rowan-berries for Grainne. Hercules killed the dragon that guarded the golden apples in the garden of the Hesperides. Such stories have been widely spread in primitive stages of human developement and retain a strong hold of the human mind in ages of more advanced civilisation. *Searbhan* s.m. dandelion; derived from *searbh*, bitter. The giant was evidently called Searbhan Lochlannach from his fierceness.

A ta in tarm sen dee gi loan. A ta an t-arm sean dith gu luan. That is its name for ever. *No ful leight*—no fuil laoigh. *Fuil laoigh*, calf's blood, is pointed to in the tale of Deirdri as being very red.

Gil a zaid na blai-feith.—Gile a dheud na blàth feith, Whiter his teeth than honeysuckle flower.

Gilcallum m yunollaig in turskail so seiss. Gille-callum Mac an Ollaimh an t-ursgeul so sios. Gilcallum, Son of the Doctor tells this tale. *Di voneis.* *Bhoineas* for *bhuineas* in Islay. *Dundealgan*, Dundalk was originally applied not to the modern town in ancient times, but to the great fortress, now called the moat of Castletown, a mile inland. There can be no doubt that this is the Dun-dealgan of the ancient histories and romances, the residence of Cuchullin, Chief of the Red Branch knights in the first century. In some of the tales of the *"Leabhar na h-Uidhre,"* it is called *Dun-Delca*, but in later authorities *Dun-Dealgan, i. e.* Dealga's fort; and according to O' Curry it received its name from Dealga, a Firbolg chief, who built it."—('Joyce's Irish Names of Places,' first series, p. 278.)

Uladh, genitive plural of *Ulaidh*. Ultonians or Ulster men. It is a people's name, not a territorial one, and according to Dr. Whitley Stokes, signifies bearded men, from *ula* beard. Ulster is formed by adding *ster*, a contraction of the Norse *stadhr*, a place, to the Gaelic name. *Forranach*, fierce; Forranach, an oppressor, a destroyer.—O' Reilly.

In the "Wooing of Emer," translated by Professor Kuno Meyer, (Archæological Review, p. 73,) it is said of Forgall:—"Forgall himself, too, hard is it to tell his many powers. He is stronger than any labourer, more learned than any druid, sharper than any poet. It will be more than all your games to fight against Forgall himself. For many powers of his have been recounted of manly deeds," said Emer to Cuchullin. In the Dean's variant *Fhorgaill* is corrupted into *Orginn.*

Gniomhaidhe an actor, an agent, a doer.—O' Reilly. *Saoradh*, deliverance. *Seang*, prudent, courteous, stately; subtle, subtile.—O' Reilly. *San* which in O' Reilly denotes holy, is the nearest word to the word in the original *sann* which is to be found in dictionaries. *Rac*, a king, a prince.—O' Reilly. In Llwyd's Comparative Vocabulary of the Original Languages of Britain, we find at p. 140, Rex Ir. *Righ*, breas, rake F. stands for O' Flaherty, *raig* in the original stands for *raic*, the vocative of *rac;* a prince or king. *Aoidhe*, a stranger; *Onnchît* a leopard. *Tarm=Do airm*, thy place occurs twice in the original, one is not a mistake for *t' ainm*, thy name. *Airm*, denoting place, occurs both in O' Reilly and in Llwyd. The quatrains 24, 25, 26, 27, 30 and 31, are from Gillies' variant of the ballad.

Airmidh, honour is found both in Llwyd and in O' Reilly. So *arrum* in the original is nearer to *airmidh* than to *urram*.

Emer the daughter of Forgall, after many adventures became the wife of Cuchullin. The ring mentioned in Gillies' variant, is explained in the "Wooing of Emer." (Archæological Review, June 1889, p. 301.)—"Cuchulaind and Aife went on the path of feats, and began combat there. Then Aife shattered Cuchulaind's weapon, so that his sword was no longer than his fist. Then Cuchulaind said—" Ah," cried he, " the charioteer of Aife, and her two horses and her chariot have fallen down in the glen and have all perished." At that Aife looked up. Then Cuchulaind approached her, seized her at her two breasts, took her on his back like a shoulder, and carried her with him to his own host. Then he threw her from him to the ground, and placed his bare sword over her. And Aife said, "Life for life, Oh Cuchulaind," "My three wishes to me," said he. "Thou shalt have them as they come from thy breath," said she. "These are my three wishes," said he, "thou to give hostage to Scathach, without ever opposing her; thou to be with me to-night before thy dun; and to bear me a son." "I promise it thus," said she. It was done in that wise. Cuchulaind then went with Aife and slept with her that night. Then Aife said that she was with child, and that she would bear a boy. "I shall send him this day seven year to Erinn," said she, "and do thou leave a name for him." Cuchulaind gave a golden finger ring for him, and said to her that he should go and seek him in Erinn when the ring would fit his finger; and that Conla was the name to be given to him, and told her that he should not make himself known to anyone; that he should not go out of the way of any man, nor refuse combat to any man. Thereupon Cuchulaind returned back again to his own people and came along the same road.

Banbha, an ancient name of Ireland.

"The Red Branch Knights of Ulster, so celebrated in our early romances, and whose renown has descended to the present day, flourished in the first century, and attained their greatest glory in the reign of Conor Mac

Nessa. They were a kind of militia in the service of the monarch, and received their name from residing in one of the houses of the palace of Emania called *Craebh-ruadh* (Creeveroe), or the Red Branch, where they were trained in valour and feats of arms. The name of this ancient military college is still preserved in that of the adjacent townland of Creeveroe; and thus has descended through another medium, to our own time, the echo of these old heroic times."—('Joyce's Irish Names of Places,' first series, p. 90.)

ARCHIBALD SINCLAIR, PRINTER AND PUBLISHER, 10 Bothwell Street, Glasgow.

www.ingramcontent.com/pod-product-compliance
Lightning Source LLC
Chambersburg PA
CBHW031109020726

47495CB00007B/2123